OLANSIA

CATHERINE BANKS

TURBO KITTEN

CHAPTER ONE

My mother never screams, even when startled, but even from two blocks away I knew the screams were hers. I raced home, hopped over the Johnson's waist-high white picket fence, narrowly missing their dachshund's teeth, and burst through the front door. I skidded to a halt on the entryway rug at the sight before me.

Facing my mother was a wolf, a real wolf. It had grey fur of varying shades and was gorgeous, and intimidating. How did it get in the house?

"Mom, what's going on?" I asked softly.

"Don't move," she ordered me and then looked at the door. "Scratch that; shut and lock the door and *then* don't move."

She was incredibly calm for having just screamed the first time in her life and facing off with a wolf, but I obeyed her. I moved slowly as I shut and locked the door and then held still as I faced the wolf. I wasn't certain locking ourselves inside with the wolf was the smartest idea, but I trusted Mom.

"How did that wolf get in here? Where the hell did it come from?" I asked her nervously.

The wolf wasn't snarling at us, thankfully, but it watched us curiously.

"Remember all those jokes and quirks your Dad said was because he was a werewolf?" she asked me.

"Yeah?" I replied and looked at the wolf. "But...no. How? What?"

The wolf's body began convulsing and bones snapped and popped as they formed a new shape, a half wolf, half man shape. "Rrr..." the wolf growled and then shook his head. "Test...testing. Ah, there we go."

It was my Dad's voice, no doubt about it.

"I'm sorry I scared you, Love," he told Mom.

"It wasn't so much you turning into a wolf that scared me as it was your bones breaking and moving under your skin," she said and walked towards him.

He nodded. "It's gross, but eventually you will get used to it."

"Doubtful," she mumbled, then stroked her fingers through his fur. They'd been together a long time and she seemed to take this in stride and assume he wouldn't hurt her. Since he was talking normally, and not snarling at her, it seemed safe to assume he was in control of himself and she was safe touching him.

"How?" I asked.

They both turned towards me and Dad said, "Two hundred years ago magic was taken from the world. We don't know why or how, but it disappeared and with it, our ability to shift forms."

"So, you really are a werewolf?" I asked, dumbfounded as I stared at the truth in front of me. Werewolves existed. My Dad was actually a werewolf. All the jokes about his possessiveness with Mom around other men and being a night person, weren't just silliness.

"I enjoyed teasing you both about it because I never imagined that you would find out the truth, but—" He motioned at himself. "Clearly magic has returned."

I looked down at my human body with a scowl. "Does this mean that I am not a werewolf?" I asked him, disappointed. As a kid, I used to howl and growl with Dad as we teased Mom he was a werewolf and I was his wolf child. I was a tomboy who spent more time with the guys in the mud than with dolls, so I loved the idea of being a werewolf.

"Did you feel the magic return?" he asked me.

"I felt a really strong warm wind blow past me and then I felt really warm inside, like after you drink a shot of alcohol, but way stronger."

He nodded. "That means you do have magic."

Mom stuck out her bottom lip in a pout. "That means I don't."

Dad's body changed again as he turned back into his normal human self. Strangely he was shredded, like he had done steroids.

Mom's eyes widened. "What..."

"With the lycanthropy properly working, I am finally looking how I should have been this whole time," he explained to her.

She smirked and pressed herself closer against him. "Thank god for lycanthropy."

I fake gagged and said, "Get a room."

Dad rolled his eyes at me and hugged Mom slowly, like he was afraid of hurting her. Maybe he was? Maybe he had increased strength now.

"You're not going to eat me or attack me in the middle of the night, right?" she asked as she laid her head on his shoulder.

He hugged her tightly and stroked his hand down her head. "No. Even in wolf form I recognize your scent, and Celwyn's, and I know instinctively that you are my mate, er, wife."

"So, if I have magic, why didn't I transform like you did?" I asked.

"After I've eaten, I will help you learn to control your powers," he promised.

I frowned and registered the fact that Dad had pants on. "How'd you keep pants on through your transformations?"

"I created them with my magic," he explained. "You have no idea how much I have missed this ability."

Mom tugged on one of the belt loops. "They feel real."

"They are real," he assured us.

"Cool," I said with a smile. "I want to be able to do that."

"If she can, that will save us a ton of money on annual clothing costs," Mom said.

I stuck my tongue out at her and she laughed in response. My reaction to all of this surprised me. Hysteria seemed a more probable reaction, yet I wasn't freaking out or scared.

"I'm going to check the perimeter. Heat me up some meat?" he asked Mom.

She kissed his cheek and headed towards the kitchen. "No peeing on the fence."

He laughed and said, "no promises," then walked out the back door.

I followed Mom into the kitchen and plopped down into a chair at the table. "A real werewolf," I whispered.

"It's crazy, right? I know I should be freaking out, but I don't know, with all the teasing and all the books I've read I—"

"And your obsession with werewolves anyway," I added.

She waved her hand dismissively. "Yes. I guess I prepared myself for this."

"I feel the same," I agreed. "Maybe that was part of his plan when teasing us."

"Well, he definitely never lied to us about it," she said and then began laughing hysterically. She bent over, clutching at her stomach as she continued to laugh.

Her laugh was infectious and soon I was bent over laughing as well.

"I pictured him peeing on the trees and growling at that little weiner dog next door," she gasped between laughs.

"I pictured him fighting over a chew toy with him," I said.

We burst into another fit of hysterics and Dad found us sitting on the floor laughing when he returned.

"Well, I'm glad you're taking this so well," he said.

"Well, it makes sense," she told him and wiped her eyes. "Just please don't poop outside. I don't want to pick up dog poop."

She and I looked at each other and our laughing fit returned.

"Ha. Ha. You're both so funny. How about you come up with something original?" he teased us.

"Wait, did you say that you're two hundred years old?" Mom asked him.

"Uh..." he said smartly.

"How can you be two hundred years old?" she asked and then paused. "Please tell me that you aren't really a clone. All those clone jokes were just jokes, right? There aren't really clones of you walking around, are there?"

"Are there really aliens?" I asked him. He used to joke that when he had random unaccounted-for wounds, they were from the aliens testing him. So many times, we would see people who looked incredibly similar to him, that we started calling them his clones.

"Slow down, one question at a time," he ordered us. "First, I need food."

"Well I need answers," Mom said. She got up and reheated the fajita meat and vegetables from last night and then tossed it into a bowl for Dad.

He scarfed it down and held out the empty bowl with a pout. She rolled her eyes and heated up the leftovers from the weekend. It took several bowls of food to fill him up, but that wasn't abnormal from his usual self.

Once satisfied, he leaned back with a contented sigh and smiled. "That was delicious."

"Okay, so are you certain that I am a werewolf?" I asked him.

"No, you may be a werewolf or you may be some other type of shifter. Shifter genes are, well, shifty. You could come from two werewolf parents and be a werelion. It's up to whoever is in charge of us all to decide."

A werelion? That sounded fun.

"Okay, what do I do first?" I asked with excitement.

"First, your mom needs to go upstairs."

"Why?" she asked and folded her arms across her chest.

"Because she may hurt you before she recognizes you in human form. She won't be able to do much damage to me, but she could rip your arm in half with one swipe," he explained.

She frowned, but walked towards the stairs. She paused in the doorway and smiled at me. "Remember that I'll love you no matter what you are or are not."

"Thanks, Mom."

She went upstairs, stomping and muttering the whole way.

"Sit down in the middle of the kitchen and close your eyes. Take deep breaths and picture a herd of antelopes running in a valley."

I followed his directions and my body began tingling.

"See me running next to you as we chase down the antelope," he continued.

Several bones separated and I screamed.

"Now, pounce on the antelope!" he ordered me.

My body exploded in a cloud of mist and then I stood in the middle of the room, taller than Dad. His eyes were wide in shock and he said, "That's not exactly what I expected to happen."

What was I? I tried to look at myself, but couldn't and there were no mirrors in the kitchen.

"Picture yourself changing into a tiger," he said. "Like the Siberian ones you loved as a kid."

I closed my eyes and did as he asked and my body exploded again. When the cloud cleared, I growled and then hissed.

"Amazing," he whispered.

I collapsed, exhausted and back in my human form. "What, what was I?" I asked breathlessly.

"First you were a stag and then you were able to turn into a Siberian Tiger."

Wow.

"So, what type of shifter am I?" I asked. Obviously, I wasn't a werewolf or a werelion.

"You are something that I never thought I would see in my lifetime again," he whispered. "You're a therianthrope."

"A therianthrope!" Mom yelled as she walked in the kitchen. "Oh, how exciting! That means she can turn into any animal she wants, right?"

Mom was a bit of a mythology and fantasy fanatic. It made growing up fun as I learned about various mythological gods and goddesses and creatures.

"Yes," Dad said.

"Are they rare?" she asked him.

He picked up a pen from the table and twirled it. "Technically they were extinct."

"Extinct? What happened?" I asked.

He looked at Mom and she said, "Just tell us."

"They were hunted into extinction. The different were-factions didn't like the idea that a Therianthrope could turn into..." he paused and then said, "...any animal and possibly infiltrate their groups. They were a very nervous and paranoid bunch."

"So, they'll kill me if they find out?" I asked sadly. Just when I get a cool ability it turns out to be life threatening.

"Possibly," he mumbled.

"If we have her only change into a wolf, will we be able to convince them that she's a werewolf?" Mom asked hopefully.

He shook his head. "She changes differently. Our bones break and shift, but her body changes magically in an instant. As soon as they saw her shift they would know what she is."

"So, what are we going to do?" Mom asked.

"For now, we are going to turn on the news to see if magic has caused chaos. We'll determine our next steps after that."

My body was depleted of energy, but I was able to pull myself up and leaned on the walls as I headed into the living room. Dad helped me to the couch and sat down, cuddled up with Mom at his side.

"You still haven't answered our questions," she reminded him in a loud whisper.

"News first, then answers."

"That's what you said about the food," she grumbled.

"Shh," he said and turned on the news.

I gasped when the first channel came on. All of the major cities were experiencing riots and chaos. One city had a guy levitating off the ground with lightning coming out of his fingertips and another had a man vomiting lava.

"I suspected as much," Dad said.

"Humans aren't great with change," Mom reminded him. "Magic being real and some being able to use it is a huge change. It's not surprising that they're a bit uncontrollable right now."

"Do you think the military is going to try to round up or wipe out those of us with powers?" I asked Dad.

He shrugged. "Probably."

"What are we going to do?" Mom asked and hugged him.

"We will figure it out in the morning. Let's get a good night's rest, since it will probably be our last night in our beds, and then we can figure everything out when we are recuperated."

I hadn't thought I would be able to sleep, but I collapsed as soon as I plopped onto my bed. After a quick change of clothes, I walked downstairs.

Mom looked like she hadn't slept at all and Dad looked rested as always. He could get two hours of sleep and look rested.

"Decision made?" I mumbled as I stumbled into the kitchen for breakfast.

"Not yet," Dad said. He lifted his pan from the stove top and expertly flipped the food around with just a flick of his wrist. I tried that move once and had spent the next twenty minutes cleaning the kitchen floor.

"When do you think you'll make a decision?" I asked. I had friends I would have to say bye to and packing to do if we were leaving.

Dad shrugged. "I'm waiting to see how things progress today. If we are leaving, it won't be until tomorrow."

"Why aren't our neighbors freaking out or rioting?" I asked Dad.

He smirked and then tilted his head towards the front door. "Go look for yourself."

I looked at Mom for a hint, but she shrugged and followed me out the front door.

I stepped outside into a world of fantasy. Mr. Johnson was levitating above his house, using wind powers to clean out his gutters. Ms. Sandson across the street turned into a wolf and lay out on her driveway in the sunlight. The Henderson Family were all throwing spheres of water at each other. Every family in our court was some type of mythological being. Had Dad known that when he bought the house here? Had everyone moved here knowing the other?

"Good morning, Mr. Johnson," Mom called and waved to him with a wide smile.

He turned and smiled at us. "Good morning! Seemed like a perfect time to clean out the gutters and mark that off my honey-do list."

"I'm sure Mrs. Johnson is happy to hear that," Mom said. "You could always pop over and do ours too, if you're bored."

He laughed and said, "You bake me some of your famous cookies and it's a deal."

Magic. Magic was real and it still hadn't completely sunk in for me.

"Come on, Cellybean. Let's get some breakfast," Mom said and guided me inside with an arm around my shoulders.

"Breakfast is ready!" Dad called.

I ate numbly through breakfast and sat in the living room with my parents as they watched the news stories. Last night had seemed more like a dream than anything, but now I had to face it fully.

"Magic exists," I whispered. "There are people with magic and people who can change shapes. I can change shapes."

"Yes," Mom said. "And Dad and I are here to help you adjust."

"Are there unicorns?" I asked.

Dad shrugged. "I've never seen any."

"Vampires?"

He nodded. "Though they aren't like the books and movies make them out."

"Trolls?"

"Yes."

"Gods and Goddesses?"

Dad sighed. "I've never really been a believer in any of them, but some swear that their powers came to them from one God or Goddess or another. Without proof, I can't call them a liar, but they don't have proof either."

This was insane. Part of me was thrilled, but the other part of me was terrified. The bad guys now might have super powers. Now they might not just kill you, but devour you or crush you.

"Ask your dad how old he is," Mom told me with a smirk.

Dad frowned at her.

"How old are you?"

"Three hundred and eighty-nine," he said.

"So, you really are an old man," I said.

"I always knew it," Mom told me.

"Wait, we have pictures of you growing up as a kid. And you were younger looking when Mom met you," I commented.

"The pictures of me growing up are fake. I haven't aged in two hundred years, but to keep up appearances I forced my body to revert with the last bit of my magic. When I met your mom and we bonded, I began aging in time with her."

"But there wasn't any magic," I reminded him.

"Magic does what it wants," he said with a shrug. "It decided that I should age with your mom."

"Does that mean that you'll die with her too?"

He sighed and squeezed Mom's hand on top of the table. "I don't know. We will see what happens as we grow older."

"Do you think we might be able to stay here?" I asked hopefully.

"Not permanently," he said. "Soon the shifters will gather and we will have to join everyone at the headquarters, wherever that might be."

"Will others have non-shifter mates?" Mom asked.

He nodded. "I'm sure of it."

"Was it allowed in the old days?" she questioned.

Mom was self-conscious and knowing that there were women who were werewolves too was only going to add her to anxiety.

"Yes," he said and looked at me. "Can you give us some time?"

I nodded and left them to talk. I put on a jacket and shoes and headed to the gang's normal spot. If I had not broken my cell phone a few days ago, I'm sure it would have been blown up with messages. I waved to the neighbors as I left the court and hurried down the creek trail to the little island we had claimed ten years ago.

The little shack we had built as kids barely stood on its own now, but we kept reinforcing it to keep it up. None of us wanted to tear it down to rebuild it, even if it would make it stronger. I hopped across the low moat and opened the door.

Nate and Ronnie sat inside, both drinking straight out of whisky bottles.

"Hey guys," I said to get their attention.

"Celwyn!" Ronnie yelled happily. He stumbled over to me and hugged me tightly. "We got worried that something had happened to you."

"I'm good, sorry for worrying you."

"Where have you been?" Nate asked and punched me lightly on the arm.

"Dad had us on lock down yesterday," I said and shrugged. "The news has been crazy."

Nate and Ronnie nodded.

"Where's everyone else?" I asked. Normally the whole crew would be here, all six of us barely fit in the shack now that we were adults, but we still managed.

"We haven't heard from any of the others," Ronnie said softly.

"What about their houses?" I asked, worried.

"Empty."

"Like furniture moved or people vacated empty?" I questioned.

"Like alien abduction empty," Nate said and took a long drink from his bottle.

"Shit," I whispered and plopped down on the bean bag chair I always sat on. I was hoping to find Orion.

Nate held out his bottle and I gladly took a few swigs.

"So, neither of you guys has magic or anything?" I asked them. "I won't judge if you do."

They both shook their heads.

"What about you?" Ronnie asked.

For some reason, I didn't want to tell them. It felt like a secret I should keep. I never kept secrets from them. "No, nothing."

"Bummer," Nate said.

"Right?" I said loudly and sighed.

At twenty-two years old, I had not done much with my life. I'd finished college last year and applied at a ton of places, but never received a call back. I was considering some type of forestry or animal warden job.

Mom liked having me at home, so I wasn't in too much of a rush. Now that the future was uncertain, I wished I had done more.

"I heard the Government is rounding up people with powers," Ronnie said softly.

My eyes widened in fear. I had suspected they might do that, but hearing that it was happening...

"Is it just a rumor or true?" I asked.

Ronnie shrugged. "The news showed the military putting people in trucks."

"It was probably the rioters," Nate said.

"Celwyn," Dad called from outside the shack.

"Got to go," I whispered and waved before walking out.

Dad stood with his eyes locked on the horizon. His jaw was clenched and his hands fisted at his sides.

"What's up?" I whispered.

"Trouble. Time to come home," he responded without shifting his gaze.

"Can you see something?"

He nodded and spun on one heel. "Home. Fast."

We sprinted home, past our neighbors who all wore worried expressions as they watched the horizon too. What was it? What did they see?

"Pack. Now," he ordered me. "Only the essentials."

With a nod, I ran up the stairs to my room. The glow in the dark stars on my ceiling brought no comfort as I packed my largest backpack with clothes, my journal, pictures I couldn't part with, and some extra pairs of shoes. It didn't take me long to add my bathroom necessities to my bag and I was once again thankful that I wasn't a girl who worried about makeup or hair styles.

Dad and Mom stood in the living room looking out the window, hand in hand. "What is it?" I whispered as I slipped my running shoes on.

"The Government," Dad growled.

"So, they are rounding us up," I gasped.

"They've likely got some of magic users in high level seats suggesting that the rest of us are high security risks," he explained.

"What are we going to do?" Mom asked nervously.

"Mr. Johnson and Mrs. Hill put up a glamour over our court to make it look abandoned. As long as they don't have someone with them who can see through it, we should be fine. Otherwise, we're going to run out the back door and head to the neighborhood across the field. We can ditch them in the other houses and I can find us a car to steal."

Time dragged as we stood, rigid and afraid, in our living room and waited to find out what would happen next.

The rumble of trucks grew louder and then I saw them. Three military flatbed trucks with tarps over the top to hide the contents, one jeep with a gun in the back, and two jeeps with military men and women drove down our court.

One of the men from the jeep stood, took off his glasses, and blinked rapidly. His eyes began to glow and then he smiled. "Nice glamour, but not good enough to hide from me."

"We can do this the nice way, where you all come out and let us examine you. Or, you can resist and many of you may be hurt in the process. We don't want to hurt you, but you need to come with us," one of the military men said.

"You can't just arrest citizens without cause," Mrs. Hill said as she walked outside.

"That stupid old bird," Dad muttered.

"We are taking those with powers in for questioning to ensure that our national security is safe," the man said.

"You two stand by the back door and wait for me," Dad said.

Mom didn't want to let go of his hand, but she took mine and followed me to the back door. The soldiers were exiting the vehicles to begin their searches. Dad watched them and then slowly backed towards us. He set his hand on the door and waited. I strained to hear what he was waiting for, but my hearing wasn't as good as his apparently.

He suddenly turned the knob and opened the door, but put an arm in front of us to stop us from exiting. He leaned his head out, sniffed twice and then picked Mom up and started running. I ran after him, thankful that our heights were similar. We crossed the field of dry grass and stopped at the fence that blocked the field from the other neighborhood.

"I can't jump over that," Mom grumbled.

"I know, baby," Dad whispered and then with one hand on the top of the fence, vaulted over the top with Mom in his arms. I heard her gasp and was very glad she wasn't a screamer.

I climbed over clumsily and landed on my butt on the ground. "That was impressive, Dad."

He smiled proudly. "Your old man still has some moves."

We walked slowly around the side of the house we had landed behind. Dad moved silently and soon we were inside a stolen car driving down the road. This neighborhood was completely vacant. The military must have come through here first.

"I need a nap. This is too stressful," Mom complained.

Dad patted her knee. "We'll be fine."

"Where are we going?" I asked. If the government was searching for people, there wasn't likely any place to hide.

"Uncle Chuck's," Dad answered.

Uncle Chuck was Dad's best friend. He was also a crazy prepper (person who hordes water and food in preparation of a disaster). Despite that, he was a ton of fun to spend time with. He had all kinds of conspiracies to talk about.

"Does he know-"

"Yes," Dad answered before I could finish. "He's not human either."

"Oh." Well, maybe that explained some of his paranoia.

"My gun is at the house," Mom pouted. She loved her rifle. She and Dad went target shooting often for fun.

"I'll buy you a new one," Dad promised.

"With a laser?" she asked.

He laughed. "Stop acting like a kid, you brat."

She straightened and said, "It' s either that or I scream like a banshee from anxiety."

"How will you know when the shifters make their headquarters?" I asked Dad.

He tapped his head. "Mental contact."

"They can contact you across the country?" I asked, my eyes widened.

"No, it gets passed along person to person. It's not something we consciously do, it's just programmed into us."

"Interesting," Mom whispered.

Dad merged with traffic, driving away from our neighborhood for possibly the last time. My friends, my life, were spent in that neighborhood. I wasn't sure I liked the idea of never seeing it again.

"Once we're at Chuck's, he is going to start training you," Dad told me. "You do what he says. He's the best shifter I've ever met."

"Okay."

"Won't he be rusty after two hundred years?" Mom asked.

Dad shook his head. "It' s like riding a bike. Once you do it again, you remember everything."

As we drew nearer the main city, we could see smoke from fires and helicopters flying overhead. "It's like the zombie apocalypse," I whispered.

"Except the Government would be right to shoot all the non-humans then," Mom said.

I laughed despite our situation and then relaxed into my seat. Maybe we would get out of this okay.

"It won't be long until they set up checkpoints. If they get a mage on their side, he could help them locate us," Dad said.

"Are planes grounded?" I asked. I had not watched the news with them or paid attention to it. I probably should have.

"All transportation is pretty much grounded," Mom answered.

"Wake me up when we're at Uncle Chuck's," I said and curled up on the backseat. I had nothing to contribute during the car ride and sleep seemed like it might be a precious commodity soon enough.

CHAPTER TWO

"Y ou lazy, brat," Chuck grumbled above me. "Get up."

I stretched and yawned. "You're lazy," I mumbled.

He grabbed my arms and dragged me out of the back of the car. I yelped in surprise and barely got my legs underneath me before hitting the dirt.

Chuck was my height, five foot eight, but incredibly buff. He looked even more ripped now. "So, you got a bulk up from the magic returning too?" I asked.

He flexed and kissed his bicep. "Yes, ma'am."

I rolled my eyes at him and tugged on his long hair. "You turning into a hippie?"

He laughed and ran a hand through his shoulder length, chestnut hair. "No, just been too busy getting ready. You know, for the Government to come searching for me and protecting you guys."

"You think they'll come searching for us?" I asked, a shudder running through me. Would they kill me? Would they hurt mom even though she didn't have magic?

He put his arm around my shoulders and squeezed. "Don't

worry, girl. Your dad and me know a thing or two to keep us alive and safe."

"I would hope so after two hundred years," I said with a smirk.

"He's actually three hundred," Dad said as he rounded the car.

"Shut up," Chuck growled.

"We're going to get our beds set up," Mom told me. "Chuck's going to start training you." She faced Chuck and pointed at him. "Don't hurt my baby or I'll skin you."

He smiled and tilted his head to look down at me. "I'm more scared of her threat than of any other mythological creature alive."

"She can be frightening," I agreed.

Dad led Mom away and Chuck headed off into the woods at the back of his compound. His compound had a ten-foot-high wood fence around the perimeter, plus thick woods surrounding his houses, hiding them from plain sight. His real residence lay underneath the ground, two floors down. I didn't really like being in there, but they assured me he had super reinforced everything.

"So, what are we going to do?" I asked him.

"He said you're a therianthrope," Chuck said.

I nodded. "That's what he said."

"First, I need to see if he is right," he told me. "And if he is, you and I are going to do a lot of self-defense training."

"Why would they kill me? I don't want to hurt anyone," I whispered. Not that I wouldn't, I would protect myself and my family if need be.

"Let's follow step one and then we will move along from there," he said.

We had walked far out into the forest, to a spot where the canopy covered a slight opening. Dad and he used to fight here sometimes for fun.

"What forms did you change into?" Chuck asked.

"Stag and tiger."

He whistled. "That's definitely a different enough pair. How about turning into a cat?"

"Okay, it might take me a minute." I closed my eyes and pictured a cute little black cat with a white spot in the center of her forehead. My body filled with warmth and then I felt it explode and shrink at the same time. I opened my eyes and blinked at the weird coloring of my surroundings with my new eyes.

Chuck squatted down to inspect me and said, "No doubt about it, kid. You're a therianthrope. Change into a bird."

After six more changes, I lay sprawled out on the forest floor, the cool leaves sticking to my face from my sweat.

"I'm impressed. You've got really good control for being a new shifter," he said as he picked me up and tossed me over one of his shoulders.

I would have complained, but I was too tired to do anything except rely on him to carry me to the house. He set me down on what would be my bed for the foreseeable future and went to the fridge.

"After a lot of changes like that, you will need to hydrate and eat," he told me.

"Okay."

"You really should only change three times in a few hours to keep from exhausting yourself."

"So, switch from human to animal to human to animal is three changes?" I asked for clarification.

"Yes."

"It's usually a good idea to keep jerky or protein bars in mass in your bag at all times. That way you can get some quick nourishment and keep yourself from being vulnerable. Rule number one in the shifter world is don't let anyone see your vulnerability."

"Sounds like a fun group," I muttered and then chugged an entire bottle of water without stopping for air.

He handed me another bottle and a protein bar. "I wasn't completely upset about being separated from them," he told me with a smile.

"Separated? I thought magic just left?" I asked, confused.

Chuck looked over at Dad and asked, "You didn't tell them?"

"About what?" Dad asked.

"Home."

Dad flinched. "No."

"Dude, they need to know the whole story," Chuck chastised him. "Alright, let's cook up some food and then we can have story time with Uncle Chuck."

Dad and Mom cooked fried potatoes, eggs, and bacon. I ate two full plates and then lay on the floor in front of Chuck's chair on my stomach, my head propped up on my hands like a child listening to a story.

"Two hundred years ago, your dad and I were living on a large island called Olansia. We lived in a place called, The Hall of Jackals, a sort of headquarters for the shifters. One week before magic disappeared, we were assigned a mission away from the island, here in the States. The next week, magic disappeared and our home disappeared as well."

"The island disappeared?" I asked in disbelief. How could an entire island disappear?

"The strongest of each of the races who lived on Olansia used their magic to send the island, and the people on it, to another dimension. They did it to keep the people and their magic safe. It stranded us here, unfortunately, and they haven't returned."

"So, you think it might return now that magic is back?" Mom guessed.

Chuck nodded his head. "It's possible."

"What would that mean if it does reappear?" I asked.

"That we'd be looking for transportation to the island," Dad answered.

"We would have to move there?" I asked. I liked the States.

"Trust me, it would be the best place for us. The humans would not be able to touch us there. It will be the safest place for those of us with magic," Chuck assured me.

"Except then I would have to worry about the others trying to kill me because of what I am," I reminded them.

"If things haven't changed much, which I doubt they have, I should be able to keep you safe," Chuck said.

"What's he mean?" Mom asked.

"Chuck was second in line of all the shifters when we were there. If he can use his title, he can grant her protection and the others should leave her alone. The issue is that there are going to be a lot of new shifters who don't know how we handle things and they are going to cause problems with the pecking order," Dad explained. "I hate the stupid politics of it all. That was a huge plus to us being left here."

"This sounds an awful lot like the books I've read," Mom mumbled with a satisfied smile.

Dad sighed and chose to not comment.

"What's our plan?" I asked. We couldn't just sit down here and wait for the government to show up.

"We're going to hide out for as long as we can, see if Olansia resurfaces, or they create another base, and then we are going to go join the rest of our clan," Chuck said.

"How long are we going to wait?" Not that I didn't enjoy being here, but I knew I would be on edge the entire time waiting for what would happen next.

"As long as it takes," Dad said. "I know it's hard, but trust me, we don't like not knowing what's going to happen either."

"I should probably give Celwyn a tour to refresh her memory so she knows where the armory and all the important things are," Chuck said.

"I'm too tired," I grumbled.

"Come on, kid. Just one quick tour and then we can come back and bunker down for bed," he promised me.

Thankfully there wasn't that much to see. Just the armory, kitchen, bathroom, infirmary, and food storage. His infirmary was pretty much a hospital with all kinds of equipment that was no doubt expensive to purchase.

"Where do you get all your money?" I asked him.

"Good investments," he said. "I purchased quite a few shares in companies when they were small that are now leaders in their industries."

"I guess it does pay to be old," I snickered.

"Har har har." He mocked me. "It only pays to be old if you're smart too."

"I always wondered why you weren't in the military, but having lycanthropy was probably a big reason, right?"

"No, I just don't like people telling me what to do when they're a tenth of my age," he replied. "I thought about joining, but the idea of some thirty-year-old puke yelling at me to do pushups was not something I could stomach."

"Would your blood work have come back different?"

He nodded. "Yeah, but they wouldn't have been able to figure out why or what the difference was. There have been a lot of shifters in the military over the years."

I stopped and leaned my shoulder against the wall of the hallway. "What happens if they don't listen to you since you've been gone so long?" I asked him softly.

He smiled and there was no warmth in it at all. In fact, it was terrifying. "Then I remind them why they need to listen to me."

"We'll protect you," Dad promised and hugged me from behind. "No one will hurt you while I'm breathing."

"You're going to need to focus on your wife," Chuck reminded him. "I guarantee there are going to be a lot of females looking for mates."

Mom chambered a shell into the shotgun she held down the hall and said, "They're going to have to go through me and Betsy here if they think they can touch my husband."

"Mate," Dad corrected her. "You should start using the proper terms."

"Does that make me your cub?" I asked with a frown.

"Naw, just their kid. Since you aren't one animal, we can't choose one name to call you," Chuck teased.

Chuck laughed loudly, the sounded reverberating around in the hallway. The sound cut off in the middle and his entire body tensed. Dad was standing, rigid, as well.

"Babe?" Mom whispered.

A rush of heat filled my body, making me gasp at the same time that Dad and Chuck shuddered.

"What was that?" I asked as I shivered.

"Olansia's back," Dad said. "The island is back."

We had to go to the above ground house to watch the news, which made Chuck very fidgety. It wasn't hard to find coverage of the island's return. Every single news station was covering it.

"We're coming to you live right now, from the Bermuda Triangle, where not more than five minutes ago, an island suddenly appeared," the news woman said.

"Can you clarify what you mean, Susan?" the news man asked.

"One second there was nothing here, and the next, a huge island appeared," she said. "I don't know how to explain it. There's no explanation from scientists or anyone else. The Navy is one hundred percent certain that this island was not here this morning."

"What does the island look like? Are there people?" the news man asked.

"For some reason electronics fail when we get close to the island. Scientists think there might be magnetic fields around it. The Bermuda Triangle has been known for ships and planes going missing through it as it is, it's not surprising that the island that shows up keeps us away too."

"Or it is magic keeping you and your cameras away," Chuck snickered.

"The Marines are preparing to deploy to the island," the news woman said.

"Alright, time to pack and head out," Chuck informed me.

"Tonight? Can't we sleep first?" I was so tired after changing so many times.

"We should rest first," Dad agreed. "We'll head out at first light and make our way."

Chuck sighed, but agreed.

"What's it like on Olansia?" Mom asked him.

"It's beautiful and deadly," Dad said. "You'll love it, sweetheart."

"Everyone to bed. Tomorrow is a big day," Chuck ordered us.

IT TOOK US LESS THAN THREE HOURS TO GET ON A TRAIN HEADED towards the Eastern Coast. Dad and Chuck used some type of magic they wouldn't explain to get us on the train and into a cabin. It was a tight fit, but sitting on a train headed towards a place where the Government wouldn't be able to get me for experiments or dissection was a great plan in my opinion. Though the people there might want to kill me. I just could not win.

Dad and Chuck kept pausing in midsentence or staring off at weird times. They said they were receiving messages from the other shifters, but I couldn't hear anything and they wouldn't tell us what was being said.

I dozed on and off, but I was too anxious and freaked out about everything to sleep solidly. I still hadn't come to grips with the fact that magic was real and that our world was being thrown into a state of upheaval with the government trying to round up all the magic users. Now we were fleeing to some unknown land that had no idea what had transpired over the last two hundred years.

"Are there castles?" I asked.

"I've always wanted to see a castle," Mom agreed.

"There were. Girls, it's been two hundred years since we have been there. They could have torn everything down and turned it into a nudist colony for all we know," Chuck teased.

"I'd rather not see any more naked dwarves in my lifetime," Dad muttered.

"Tickets," a man called as he walked down the aisle.

"I got it," Chuck said and stepped outside, shutting the cabin closed behind him. I strained to listen, but he spoke quietly and the door muffled the words even more. He came back inside a moment later and the man moved on to the next set of rooms. "You get next," he told Dad.

"Eat something," Dad ordered him.

Chuck snorted dismissively and closed his eyes as he leaned against the door. "I'm fine."

"How long will we be on the train?" I asked.

"She asks a lot of questions," Chuck complained.

"What else am I supposed to do?" I snapped.

"Sit back and let the adults handle it," he growled.

"Chuck," Mom warned.

"No, he's right," Dad agreed. "I know you don't like not being in control, but you're going to have to just trust us and do as we say."

"I have been. I just hoped you could give us some more information."

"We're going to ride this train as far as we can, then get off and get a boat to take us to the island."

"I thought the boats couldn't make it to the island?"

"Boats with humans can't make it, but boats with Olansians can make it."

Instead of pissing them off by asking more questions, I obeyed and stayed silent the rest of the trip. It took them longer than they planned to find a boat, but again they managed somehow and we set sail for Olansia. The boat was small, closer to a skiff than anything, but it floated and we all fit on it without tipping it over. Mom's hands clenched the bench she sat on and no matter how much Dad tried to calm her, she would not loosen her grip. I didn't blame her. I didn't like the ocean either. Well, I liked the ocean, just not the large animals that lived in it and had every right to eat us for invading their home.

A thick blanket of fog wrapped around the island, blocking it from view.

"He's being dramatic like always," Chuck grumbled.

"Who?"

"The High Mage," Dad answered. "The most powerful of the mages. He is known for his dramatics and fog was one of his favorite tricks."

"If he had been with us, he would have taken over Hollywood," Chuck whispered.

"He would have destroyed it," Dad said.

"Who goes there?" a deep voice called out.

"Members of the Hall of Jackals!" Chuck called back.

"One of you is not Olansian," the voice replied.

"She's my mate," Dad growled.

"Proceed."

I squinted my eyes, scanning the fog in front of us in search of where the voice came from, but had zero luck.

Our boat hit land and Mom hissed in surprise. Dad and Chuck jumped out into the water and pulled the boat on shore before helping us out of the boat. The fog around us cleared and revealed a large wooden fortress.

"Welcome to the Hall of Jackals," Chuck whispered in my ear. "Home sweet home."

He draped his arm across my shoulders and led me inside the front gates, their open doors like a mouth waiting to swallow me whole. A tall, slender woman with hair down to her ankles glided up to us and bowed. "Welcome, friends. We are pleased to have new brothers and sisters among us."

"Astrid," Chuck said softly. "Is that you?"

The woman straightened and gasped. "Charles?"

Charles? I guess Chuck was short for Charles.

Chuck released me and wrapped the woman in a tight embrace. Tears slipped down her cheeks as she hugged him. "I thought the worst, she whispered.

He pulled back and wiped her face. "For shame, little sister. You know no mortal can kill me."

"Who is this?" she asked and looked over at me.

Dad put his arm around my shoulders, pulling me and Mom against each of his sides. "This is my family."

She gasped. "Tyren! You mated!"

He nodded. "Astrid. I would like you to meet my mate, Lily, and my pup, Celwyn."

She rushed forward and hugged Mom and me. "I am happier to see you now that I know who you are! I long hoped this sour old dog would find a mate."

"It's nice to meet you," Mom said with a smirk at dad.

"Your pup is beautiful," Astrid said and smiled at me. "Are you a wolf like your father?"

"I, uh…" I looked at Chuck nervously. She seemed to be a friend, but I didn't know who I could tell.

"Who's Alpha?" Chuck asked her.

"Such little faith in me even after one hundred years together?" a rumbling male voice asked from behind me.

His voice made me feel safe and terrified at the same time.

"Not a lack of faith, but a question that I worried about the answer to," Chuck replied with a smile.

The man who walked out was unimposing in every way except for a feeling that surrounded him. He was one of those guys that you just knew would go crazy and tear someone apart. I knew a few guys like him in town, my best friend was like that too.

"I've maintained my Alpha status," the man said.

"Good to hear, Merle," Chuck said and clasped hands with him.

Merle returned his smile and then turned towards me. "Who are you, child?"

"She's under my protection," Chuck told him with a soft growl.

Merle's eyes widened and he turned to face Chuck. "Your protection? Is she yours?"

"She's my pup," Dad said.

"Then why…" he started to ask and turned towards me again.

"Am I still Second?" Chuck asked.

"Yes," Merle answered as he continued to stare at me.

"Then I place this child under my protection. Any who wish her harm must first fight and defeat me," Chuck said.

"What's this about?" Astrid asked nervously.

The Alpha walked around me and then drew in a long breath near my side. "Is she…"

"Perhaps we can discuss this in your private chambers?" Chuck suggested.

"I think that would be best," Merle agreed.

Chuck jerked his head to the side for me to follow him. I obeyed, keeping close to him as we entered a stone building reminiscent of a castle keep. People bowed their heads as the Alpha walked by or dropped to one knee. What did one have to do to become Alpha of the shifters? I would have to ask Chuck later.

There were all kinds of people, every race and age, walking around and talking together.

"Here, people aren't discriminated against for their skin color, but for the animal they shift into or for being a shifter versus a mage," Dad whispered to me and Mom.

"I think I prefer that," I admitted.

We walked into a room with a thick wooden door that was reinforced with steel and had a large steel ring for a handle. The room was larger than average, about the size of our living room back home. A large four poster bed took up one wall and the rest was taken up with a dresser, couch, and two velvet chairs in front of the largest fireplace I had ever seen.

Merle turned the chairs around to face the couch and sat in one. Astrid sat beside him, Mom and I sat on the couch, and Dad and Chuck stood on either side of us.

"Fill us in," Chuck requested.

"The Celestial Tigers felt a disturbance and worried that something was going to happen. They used their combined powers to send Olansia to another dimension to keep us safe," Merle explained.

Who were the Celestial Tigers?

"We have been trying for the last two hundred years to figure out a way to return, but nothing was successful," he continued.

"How did you return then?" Dad asked.

"We don't know," Merle admitted.

"We didn't cause it," Astrid answered.

"Has power changed or any major events?" Chuck asked.

Merle sighed. "How do I sum up two hundred years in a matter of minutes?"

"The Mages have grown in numbers exponentially. They dominate the South. The Demons are dwindling in number. The Fey are few and no longer breeding, if rumors are to be believed. And our numbers are half what they were when you left," Astrid explained.

"All the races lost numbers except the Mages? That seems a bit odd," Mom commented.

"They're the closest to human and are able to reproduce much faster," Merle told her.

"Tell us of this world," Astrid asked with bright, eager eyes.

"Technology has exploded in the last two hundred years," Dad said. "Their militaries far surpass ours. Instead of bows and arrows, they have devices that allow them to shoot small metal balls hundreds of feet per second. Metal contraptions that allow them to fly through the air faster than dragons and release missiles that do more damage than a flight of dragons."

Merle's eyes had widened in shock and now he sat in stunned silence.

"What of this girl?" Astrid asked.

Merle looked up at me and frowned. "She's a Therianthrope, isn't she?"

Chuck nodded. "Yes."

"You know our laws," Merle whispered.

"They are all dead. She is the only one. She won't betray us. She's like a daughter to me," Chuck told him angrily.

"How powerful is she?" Merle asked.

"Very," Chuck whispered sadly.

"Can she shift her human appearance?" Astrid asked.

"What?" I asked in shock. "That's possible? I thought I could only choose animal forms?"

"We had not tried," Dad said.

"Try to shift into your mother," Merle ordered me.

"I, uh, how…" I stuttered.

"Like with your animal forms, just close your eyes and picture the form you wish to take, in this case your mom," Chuck coached.

I stood and obeyed. Disobeying Merle seemed like a very bad idea. My body didn't explode this time, but rippled in a very unpleasant way. When I opened my eyes, everyone wore the same grim expressions on their faces.

"They will not accept her," Astrid whispered.

"We will make them," Chuck growled.

"If Adbalh discovers she exists," Merle spoke softly with his fists clenched in front of his mouth, "He will hunt her down."

"He's been hunting us for centuries already," Chuck said.

"He will do whatever he can to get her," Astrid whispered, "He's been bored these past two hundred years and she will be a new challenge."

"We could send her to the Mages," Merle suggested.

"They'd experiment on her, torture her," Dad snapped.

"The new children coming from this world will not know to be prejudiced against her," Chuck said, "She will be most likely to succeed with them."

"I cannot give her my protection," Merle said softly. He looked at me and I felt the sorrow dripping from him. "I wish I could, but I must not lose face in these times of change."

"I understand," I said and smiled. "I'm stronger than you think. I may prove you all wrong and live longer than everyone in this room."

Merle smirked and looked at Dad. "She's got your spunk, Tyren. Alright, child…what's your name?"

"Celwyn," I answered.

"Alright, Celwyn. I will grant you a chance to live. You will join the new shifters in training and hopefully your spunk will get you through," Merle said.

"Thank you," Chuck sighed loudly and ran a hand through his hair. "Thank you, Merle."

"How many have arrived?" Dad asked.

"Only a handful so far. There are about a dozen more on their way. Everyone should be here by tomorrow evening," Astrid answered.

"What happens once everyone arrives?" Mom asked.

Merle seemed to finally notice her. "I'm sorry. I was preoccupied with your daughter. Tyren, introductions please."

"Merle, this is my mate Lily. Lily, this is Merle, Alpha of the Shifters," Dad introduced.

Merle smiled and said, "Welcome, Lily."

"You should probably mark her soon," Chuck whispered.

"Or turn her," Astrid suggested.

"No," Dad snapped. "She will not be turned."

"Why not?" Mom asked.

"Because the survival rate of females being turned is ten percent," Chuck answered for Dad. "And he would rather you were alive than a shifter."

"What he said," Dad agreed.

"What does marking me consist of?" she asked.

"A bite and a scratch," Merle said.

"That you will be unconscious from for a full day afterwards," Chuck mumbled.

"Once Celwyn is settled, I will mark her. Does that work?" Dad asked Merle.

Merle nodded. "Yes, I will allow the delay."

"Have you given our rooms away?" Chuck asked.

"Of course not," Merle said and stood. "Let's get you settled."

"Chuck, can you take care of Celwyn?" Dad asked.

Chuck draped his arm across my shoulders and smiled. "Of course."

Dad took Mom's hand and led her out of the room. Mom waved to me before leaving. I didn't even have enough time to raise my hand to reciprocate the gesture.

"Come on, kid. You'll love it here," Chuck promised.

"Why did Dad take off like that?" I asked sadly.

"He's going to be on edge until he marks your mom," Merle answered. "As it stands, any other male could lay a claim to her."

"But they're mates," I replied.

"No, they've just slept together. Until he marks her, she's not technically his," Astrid explained.

"Oh."

Chuck pulled me along as we walked down hallways, through rooms of shifters gossiping, to a long narrow hallway with door after door. "These are the quarters for those of us who live here permanently," Chuck explained.

"How many of you live here usually?" I questioned. There seemed to be no end to the hallway.

"About fifty," Chuck said.

"Currently twenty," Merle corrected.

"So few?" Chuck whispered in shock.

"It's been a rough two centuries," Astrid said softly.

"Have the Demons been causing trouble?" Chuck asked.

Merle shook his head. "Actually, they've holed up in their headquarters, cut off from the rest of the island."

"Why?" I asked.

Astrid shrugged. "We aren't sure."

"Here we are," Chuck said finally and stopped in front of a door.

"You don't expect her to share your room, do you?" Astrid asked.

"She can use the room beside Chuck's," Merle said. "Come, Celwyn, let me show you your room."

"Just yell if you need me," Chuck said before going into his room with Astrid.

"Are they…"

"No, they're siblings," Merle corrected.

"Oh."

Merle opened the door to the room and motioned me inside. I stepped in and he stopped in the doorway. "As Alpha I must tell you one thing, Celwyn."

"Okay?" I said nervously.

"Though you may have no intention of betraying us now," he

began. His eyes started glowing and I felt the hairs on the base of my neck raise. "If you should betray us any time in the future, I will personally end your life. Are we clear?"

Oh yea, we were clear. "Yes, sir."

He smiled and the aura around him cleared. "Great. I hope you enjoy yourself in your new home."

After he left, I collapsed on the bed and tried to calm my racing heart. He was so terrifying. I would have to work hard and prove to them that I was an asset to the shifters. It couldn't be that hard to fit in, could it?

CHAPTER THREE

I stayed in my room until we were ordered to meet two days later. Chuck walked next to me, his clothes now leathers and two curved knives on his sides. He looked deadly and scary, which I was pretty certain was what he was going for.

"You could smile every now and then," I teased him. Chuck had always told me jokes and laughed constantly, even when discussing conspiracy theories with Dad.

"There is a time and place for lightheartedness. This is neither the place nor the time," he whispered. "This is a time and place for me to remind everyone why I am Second and not to try to double cross me." He looked down at me and said, "And to remind them why they do not want to test my patience and harm you."

Okay. Point taken. The room was filled with men and women and several teenagers. There were a couple kids that looked to be elementary school aged, but not many and zero babies. I searched for Mom and Dad, but couldn't see them. Were they here? Or had Dad forced her to stay in their room to keep her safe and away from the other males until he marked her?

Merle and Astrid stood in the front of the room and when he raised his hand the room silenced.

"Welcome, Shifters. I know many of you are unfamiliar with this island and who I am. I am Merle, Alpha of the Shifters. I am your leader and though I am merciful on occasion, you will not want to test my patience."

"I am Astrid, Alpha Female of the Shifters. You males will do well to remember that though I am female, I outrank you. I will not tolerate insubordination and I will punish you quickly and fiercely."

The room was silent as she spoke and I made a mental note to never cross her. She was a force.

"Charles," Merle called.

Chuck walked through the crowd, which parted for him, and I followed on his heels, eyes down as he had instructed. He stopped in front of Merle and knelt on one knee. I knelt on both knees behind Chuck.

"Charles, I appoint you Second," Merle said. Several people murmured in shock in the crowd, but the silence soon returned. Chuck stood up and after tapping my head, I stood as well. "As Second, Charles' word is as good as mine and he will act on my orders."

"Thank you, Alpha," Chuck said and bowed his head with his fist over his heart.

"Address the Pack," Merle ordered him.

Chuck faced the room and his eyes lit with an inner fire as he looked at each person. "I only have one thing to say. This girl beside me is under my protection. Any who wish to cause her harm must first challenge and defeat me. If you harm her, I will return your attack tenfold. Clear?"

"Clear, Second!" Most of the crowd replied immediately. Several of the people looked around nervously. They had to be newcomers, like me.

"Tomorrow the new shifters will begin their training," Merle said, "Tonight, let's enjoy a feast together as a pack. United after two centuries apart."

Everyone cheered and filed out to the dining hall. Chuck stayed beside me, his gaze sweeping over the crowd and pinning anyone who came too close to me for his comfort. A trio of men waited for him inside the dining hall.

"Charles, you old dog. I thought you had died," one of them said with a smirk.

"I'm a bit harder to kill than you might think," Chuck replied with a smirk. He clasped forearms with each of the men.

"And what is your name?" the man who had spoken asked me.

"Celwyn."

"She your pup?" he asked Chuck.

"No, she's Tyren's."

"Tyren? He's here?" one of the other men asked and looked around.

"He is."

"So, the Devil Hound finally found a mate? I never thought I would see the day," the third man who had been silent so far asked.

"She's his equal in every way," Chuck said with a wide smile.

"Then I expect great things from you," the first man said with a smile at me.

DINNER TOOK FOREVER AND BY THE TIME IT WAS OVER, I WAS TOO tired to do anything other than shambled to my room and sleep. Chuck woke me early the next morning and gave me a stack of new clothes. They were a strange material, nothing I had ever seen in the States, but comfortable and easy to move in.

We walked side by side down the hallway and his expression was even more grim than the previous night's.

"Is everything okay?" I asked him softly.

He nodded once. "Just worried."

"I can handle myself," I assured him.

"Life is different here than in the States," he reminded me. "It's dog eat dog, pretty literally."

"So, give me a run down on the rules," I requested.

"If you step out of line with someone who is a higher rank than you, they are within their rights to punish you, even kill you depending on what you did."

"How do I know what rank someone is? How will I know if they rank higher than me or not?"

"The teenagers you will learn with will develop their own ranking. It won't be obvious at first because they'll test each other out. Try to keep your head high and not back down if pressed by them. If you don't think you can win a fight against them, then dipped your chin down and take a step away from them. That will let them know that you accept them as more dominant than you."

"What if I don't want them to be more dominant than me?"

"Then you better hope you can win the fight against them."

"Will I always be fighting?"

"Not always, but the first week will most likely be daily fights."

"Okay, what else?"

"Males and females are ranked together, but also separate. If a female is ranked fifth in the pack, but second in the females, then to you she is second, while to me she is fifth. If a male ranks higher than a female and they are mated, she gains his rank because he can defend her."

"Good to know."

"If someone is close to killing you, you are free to use my name and title to get them to back off. That does not mean you can instigate fights with people you know you can't win against because you can use me to make them back off. You understand?"

"Yes, I make my bed and lie in it," I replied.

He nodded and smirked a bit. "You're a smart girl. I know you'll make us proud."

"Will I see you?"

"Not for a few weeks," he admitted.

I stopped and hugged him tightly. "Thank you."

"Show them what you're made of. Make them fear you as they fear me. Okay?"

I nodded and we continued to the back of the fortress where all the new Shifters were ordered to gather. There were eight other Shifters around my age, three females and five males. Two of the females looked terrified and stood close together. The other female stood confidently, examining her fingernails. She was muscular, athletic built, and reminded me of the gymnasts back home. The five males were a variety, short, tall, thin, muscular, fat.

One of the males who had spoken to Chuck the night of the feast was in the front of them all. He nodded at Chuck and straightened. "Attention, class."

All of us turned our attention to him. Chuck walked up next to him. "Listen to your instructor and learn well, Shifters," Chuck told us. He patted the man on his shoulder and left. "I leave them in your paws."

I watched him go and felt my heart beat quicken. With him gone, I was alone. Alone with people I did not know who grew claws and fangs.

I could as well.

I still felt nervous.

Maybe I should go cower with the other two.

"I am Mauricio," the man introduced himself. "And I will be your instructor for the next three weeks. Take a look at each other, you are going to be living and sleeping together for the next three weeks. You will develop friendships that will last hundreds of years here as well as hatreds. Choose well which you develop. Now, let's begin with the basics."

I listened intently as he explained the inner workings of the Shifters and the separate clans, each animal had their own clan with their own hierarchy. I felt like there should be a ladder of power somewhere to help those of us who would have trouble remembering so many people and their places within each clan and the Shifters as a whole.

There weren't very many rules, but the newest rule was that no one could leave the Island. I hadn't planned to leave, but being ordered to stay here made it feel more like a prison than a safe place.

"Hi, I'm Anastacia," the athletic girl said at lunch as she sat next to me.

I held out my hand with a smile. "Celwyn."

She shook it and then tilted her head at the two cowering girls. "Should we invite them over so they stop cowering?"

I nodded.

"Girls, come sit with us. We won't bite you," she called.

The girls looked at each other and then slowly sat across from us at the table.

"What are your names?" I asked them softly.

"Cecilia," the raven haired one on the left answered.

"Maria," the brown haired one said.

"It's nice to meet you both. I'm Celwyn," I replied with my best smile.

"Is it okay to speak to you?" Maria asked nervously.

I frowned. "Why wouldn't it be?"

"The Second..." Cecilia began, but then bit her lip.

"It was a bit strange that he made a point of saying you are under his protection," Anastacia said.

"It's because I'm not his blood," I answered vaguely. It was partly true.

"Are you his mate?" Cecilia asked.

I laughed. "No, he's like a second father to me."

"Oh."

"So we can talk…"

"Yes. He just wanted to make sure no one tried to hurt me. He's overprotective."

"It must be nice having someone who cares," Cecilia said softly.

The way she said it, all of us turned to look at her.

She blushed and looked down at her plate of food.

"We are orphans," Maria whispered, "From a place that used us as slave labor from a very young age."

I knew things like that existed in other parts of the world, but my bubble kept me safe from experiencing that.

"I'm sorry that you had to endure that," I whispered sincerely. "We promise not to let that happen to you ever again."

Cecilia sniffed and wiped her eyes. "Do not make promises you cannot keep."

"I promise to try my hardest to keep you safe," I told her. "Okay?"

She nodded and we all ate in silence. The boys were huddled together whispering as they ate, but I tried my hardest to ignore them. I had no interest in starting a relationship any time soon.

"Your bread roll tomorrow says they are trying to decide which one of them is going to approach our group first," Anastacia whispered.

I giggled. "I can't take that bet because I agree with you."

"How old are you?" Maria asked me.

"Twenty-two. You?"

"We are nineteen," Maria answered.

"I'm eighteen," Anastacia said.

"Great, I'm the old hag of the group."

Cecilia snickered and then covered her mouth. Anastacia laughed loudly and soon all of us were laughing. The boys looked at us curiously, but none of them approached or asked what we were laughing about.

"At least you do not look old," Cecilia said. "We had a girl in the orphanage who says she was eighteen, but she looked closer to thirty."

I cringed. "That would suck way worse than just being older."

"You're not that much older," Anastacia said. "So, it's not so bad."

"I guess you're right. Too bad my good lucks won't get me through life now that we are Shifters."

Anastacia sighed. "Don't I know it. I was living the life, getting free stuff from stupid men all the time. Now… Now I'm going to have to fight my way up the ranks."

"You wish to be Alpha?" Maria asked her.

Anastacia smiled and it was not a pleasant one. "In time, yes. I know that is not likely to happen for a couple decades at least, but I will bide my time."

"I just hope I'm not the bottom," Cecilia whispered.

"Then you better start holding your head up," I told her seriously. "Stop looking down all the time."

"It's hard to overcome what has been beaten into you most of your life," she snapped.

"Easy," I whispered, "I wasn't trying to be rude. I was just giving you some advice. I'm sorry if I upset you."

She exhaled and nodded. "It's okay. I'm just on edge."

"We all are," Anastacia agreed.

"So, ladies," one of the guys, the fat one, greeted us. "How's everyone doing?"

"Fine," Anastacia said. "So, you picked the short straw?"

Cecilia and Maria giggled softly.

He shrugged. "Who wouldn't want to come talk to some beautiful ladies?"

"Flattery will only get you so far," Anastacia warned him.

He sat down beside her and smiled, charm saturating his face. "Then I should work on improving that."

"Break is over!" Mauricio called. "Time for some shifting."

I swallowed nervously and felt my palms dampen. This was

what I was afraid of. Did Mauricio know? Why did we have to shift so soon?

We walked outside and he ordered us to split up by animal. I stood alone and fiddled with the hem of my shirt.

"Celwyn," Maria whispered, "What are you doing?"

Mauricio looked over at me and smiled. "So it is true?"

I nodded. "Yes, sir."

"Now I know why he did what he did," he muttered.

"Where should I stand?" I asked.

"There is perfect," he told me.

Everyone was looking at me and it made me fidget even more. I hated being singled out.

"Alright, wolves you are up first. One at a time I want you to shift into animal form," he ordered them.

Half of the group were wolves, including Maria and Cecilia. They all shifted, Cecilia taking a bit longer than the rest.

"Good," Mauricio called. "Now switch back to human." They obeyed and he turned his attention to the line with Anastacia. "Felines, shift." All of them except Anastacia shifted. He looked at her and arched an eyebrow. "Bear?"

She nodded.

"Shift," he instructed her.

She shifted into a beautiful bear with a white stripe across her chest.

"Beautiful," I whispered.

She stood a bit straighter after my comment and huffed.

"Shift back," he ordered that line and turned to face me. "What would you like to shift into?"

"Um, I've only shifted a few times," I admitted to him.

He nodded. "That's the same for the others. Is there an animal you liked as a child?"

"Foxes," I whispered.

He waved his hand. "Then turn into one."

"Why is he asking her what she wants to be?" one of the males asked.

I closed my eyes, trying to block out the others and shifted.

"Excellent," Mauricio whispered. "Try a hawk."

I had only done a bird once before, but hadn't flown after shifting. I shifted into a hawk and screeched before flying up into the air. The wind felt so good on my wings.

"Shift back!" he ordered me.

I shifted and fell a couple feet to the ground, landing on my knees.

"Being a bird is a much harder task," he informed me, "Their brains are small and it can overpower your human one."

"Good to know," I huffed.

"I thought Shifters could only have one animal form?" one of the males asked.

"She's unique," Mauricio informed them. "She is what is called a Therianthrope."

"My father told me about them," the fat kid said. "He said they were extinct because they could turn into people and they were too treacherous to keep around."

"Yes, they were all exterminated because of that, but with Celwyn on our side, we are confident that she will be an asset instead of a problem," Mauricio explained.

"So, she can shift her human appearance?" Anastacia asked softly.

"Yes, into anyone she wants," Mauricio told them.

Great, just tell them all my secrets. You big jerk.

"Would you like to demonstrate?" Mauricio asked me.

I shook my head. "No, I don't like shifting my human appearance. It feels wrong."

He nodded his head. "Very well. We'll work you up to that."

The rest of the afternoon I caught my teammates looking at me out of the corner of my eyes. Their expressions were either fearful or intrigued. Anastacia's expression worried me the most, she looked at me like I was a threat.

When we went to our rooms that night, no one spoke to me. I tried not to let it get to me, but it was hard. They had wanted to be friends and now, now they didn't want to talk to me.

"Self-defense time," Mauricio told us the next day. "Pair up and practice the following moves."

I expected one of the girls to pair up with me, but instead it was one of the males. He held out his hand. "I'm Sven."

I shook his head. "Celwyn."

We practiced the moves Mauricio showed us in silence and I found that I actually enjoyed these practices. I was sweating when we finally finished and drank a full bottle of water.

"You're a pretty fast learner," Sven complimented me.

"Thanks. You seem like this is old news to you."

He nodded. "My father always hoped Olansia would come back. So, he taught me to fight with my hands, sword, and had me watch videos of wolves fighting for when I was able to shift."

"I wish my dad had warned me about all this," I admitted to him.

"I could have been a bear though," he reminded me. "It is all up to the Gods what gift you get."

"Or curse," I muttered.

"I think yours is the best gift. With it, you can be a secret spy, sneak into the Government and help keep us safe. You're like that blue girl from the mutant movies," he said with a smile.

"Didn't she turn out to be a bad guy?" Anastacia asked as she walked by.

Two of the guys nearby laughed and I clenched my jaw in anger. What was her problem? She wanted to be friends before, but all of a sudden she hates me?

"Good thing that I am not her then, right?" I said.

She shrugged. "Time will tell."

"Girls, no cat fights allowed," Mauricio called.

"As if I could fight her," Anastacia said. "She's got the Second protecting her. Maybe he is in on it too. Maybe he is planning to overthrow the Alpha and will use her to…"

Anastacia was suddenly on her back and my hand was around her throat. I had not even realized that I had moved. I leaned down until our noses almost touched and said, "Do not talk about Charles that way. You know nothing about him."

"That's enough," Merle called.

I jumped away from her and dropped to one knee. "I'm sorry."

He tapped my head as he walked by. "Don't apologize for protecting your friend's honor." He stopped in front of Anastacia and squatted down until he was eye level with her where she was sitting. "Since you are young and new, I will allow this to pass. In the future, you would be wise not to make such strong accusations when you have no proof. Charles would be well within his rights to kill you for trying to sully his name like that. Celwyn would be within her rights as his charge to punish you on his behalf. Do you understand?"

She nodded her head and swallowed hard. "Yes, Alpha."

He patted her head once. "Good. Now, try and make up. It's not good for there to be animosity between you already. Celwyn is a nice girl and I promise that she is not here to be a spy or hurt any of you."

He walked away and as soon as he was gone, Anastacia stood up and glared at me. "I'll be keeping my eye on you."

"Stalker," I said in a sing song voice.

Many of the others snickered, but she glared at me and walked away. Merle wanted us to make up, but I didn't have time for her childish games. I needed to learn to protect myself and find a way to work my way up the hierarchy so that Chuck wouldn't have to protect me all the time. I needed to fend for myself. I was the strongest girl back in our town. I could be the strongest here, if I just put my mind to it. I had a unique gift that no one else had. I just had to figure out how to use it to my advantage.

The new few days didn't go much better, but the other students had stopped shying away from me in fear. Anastacia had gained a following of a few boys and whenever I looked at them, I caught them whispering while looking at me with sour expressions. It was more than enough to make me paranoid.

"Today we are going on a little trip," Mauricio told us.

"Where to?" Brent, one of the males, asked.

"To the mainland of Olansia."

"Wait, aren't we on Olansia?"

"We're on a small crescent shaped island right next to it, but we are not on the mainland. So, we are going to head over there and let you have a bit of free space to run around on," He explained.

"Any chance to get away from this place is a good idea to me," Maria whispered beside me.

I had to agree. Being cooped up at the Hall was getting old really quick. I needed some change, something new to see. Thank goodness we were getting that.

"Pack light," Mauricio ordered us, "and meet me at the dock in one hour."

I packed quickly and met up with Maria and Cecilia before heading down to the docks. They were both smiling happily, looking up for once. It made me relax even more to see them like that.

We lined up on a ship, that was really just a floating dock attached to a chain that went from the mainland to the small island we were on. Two massively muscular males used long poles to push us along the chain. There were no rails of any kind, so we all hunkered together in the center to avoid falling overboard.

"You're going to be in charge of finding your own food," Mauricio clarified. "I'll be back in three days to pick you all up.

Make sure that you survive. I'd hate to have to explain to the Alpha that one of you idiots picked a fight with a badger that you couldn't win."

A few of us snickered, but I got the feeling that the comment might have been directed at me and Anastacia. I was going to do everything that I could to stay away from her, but if push came to shove, I would not back down.

The ship hit land and Mauricio yelled at us to disembark. As soon as the last of us were off, the two males and Mauricio began their trip back. "Three days!" Mauricio called before disappearing into a thick blanket of fog that descended like a blanket thrown over a bird's cage.

"The fog moves too fast for my liking," Brent whispered next to me.

I nodded. "It's disturbing."

"We better find somewhere to make camp," Carlton said. He was always taking charge when we had to do things as groups. He was a decent leader, so I didn't mind following his orders.

We all walked together, everyone scanning our surroundings for impending threats or anything useful. Sadly, there were no houses or cabins we could use. We traveled for what felt like an hour across an empty plain until we finally found trees and then a forest. The males did a quick perimeter sweep and then we began clearing debris to lay our bedrolls down.

"Did anyone bring food with them?" Sven asked. He had started off overweight, but now he was as muscular as Carlton.

"I brought two bread rolls," I said as I laid out my bedroll. It had taken me a while to clear out the debris because the spot I had chosen was pretty rocky.

"I have a couple bottles of water," Maria replied.

"I brought some jerky," Carlton offered.

"That's not enough for all of us to share," Anastacia pointed out.

"Anyone have experience hunting?" Carlton asked.

"We can make small snare traps," Cecilia offered. "They will only be able to catch something up to the size of a rabbit though."

"That will be a good start," Carlton said.

"Let's go find a place a bit away from camp to make them," I told the two girls. "I'll come with you so I can learn how to make them too."

"I'll go with you in case there's trouble," Sven offered.

Carlton nodded his head in agreement and pulled out a pocket knife to start working on a branch he had broken. I thought about pointing out they any of us could shift into an animal with claws to kill food, but chose to keep my mouth shut and not give Anastacia a chance to make a rude comment.

I was pretty certain Mauricio wanted us to learn to hunt as animals, but I couldn't be sure.

We walked until the noise from camp was a faint whisper and then sat on the ground in a circle together. Cecilia was very skilled, her fingers moving deftly and quickly to make snares. I tried and failed several times to make one, but there wasn't much need because they set up several in the amount of time it took me to finally make one half way decent one. I would have felt bad, but Sven was having just as hard a time as I was.

"We'll check them in the morning," Cecilia explained.

"How did you learn to make these?" Sven asked them.

Cecilia looked down at her feet and pink bloomed on her cheeks. "We didn't have much food and had to find ways of catching some," she answered vaguely.

What she didn't explain was that it hadn't been for rabbits, but for rats at the orphanage.

"Looks like you managed to gain one good skill from that hellhole," I said with a bright smile.

Cecilia looked up and her embarrassment melted a little. "I guess so."

I split one roll into four pieces and shared it with Cecilia, Maria, and Sven and then tossed the other one to Anastacia.

"Why are you giving me this?" she asked.

"Because I have a piece and I'm sharing with you," I answered with what I hoped was a real smile.

"Is it safe to eat?" she asked.

I sighed and said, "Anastacia, I'm sorry that we got off on the wrong foot. I want us to be friends, not enemies. Consider it a peace offering."

She sniffed it once and then took a bite. "Thank you." She tossed the other half to Carlton who split it with two others.

"What are we going to do about drinking water?" Sven asked Carlton.

"I don't think animal get sick like humans do if they drink from a creek or river that's moving. If we shift into our animal forms to drink from a stream that isn't stagnant, we should be fine," he explained.

I hoped he was right. I really didn't enjoy the idea of having the runs in the forest with no toilet paper or bathrooms nearby.

"Isn't the Werewood Forest near here?" Cecilia asked nervously.

"What's the Werewood Forest?" I asked.

"It's the scariest forest in the world. Supposedly all of the horror films depicting haunted forests were based on this one. It's in the Demon's territory."

"Sounds fun," I said with a wicked smile.

"Like you would last more than half an hour in there," Anastacia taunted.

"Please, I could last a full day and night, no problem. I'm not afraid of anything," I bragged.

Anastacia's eyebrows furrowed and her lips pursed. "Really? You're not afraid of anything?"

I shrugged. "Nothing that I've seen or heard of yet."

"I'll make you a deal," Anastacia said. "You spend one full day and night in the Werewood Forest and I will never doubt your loyalty again. I'll even stick up for you if someone insinuates you might turn on us later."

Part of me felt like this was a trap, but I needed to make alliances and friends. I really wanted to have friends.

"Don't do it," Maria whispered urgently.

"Deal," I said and held out my hand.

Anastacia grinned wickedly and shook hands with me.

"Alright, let's hit the hay," Carlton ordered.

Normally I would have wanted to tell him to shove it, but maybe it was the animal part of me that knew we were pack and he was more dominant because I just accepted his order and went to sleep.

We lucked out and caught three rabbits the next morning for breakfast. I had to plug my ears when they killed the poor bunnies and took a long walk while they prepared them for cooking. I wasn't squeamish, but that didn't mean that I wanted to watch what they were doing. I hunted for berries or nuts of some kind, but the trees were all pines and I didn't think pinecones could make any type of edible meal.

"Hiding while they slice up the rabbits?" Anastacia asked.

I looked up in surprise, not having heard her approach. "Yeah."

"I'm not surprised. Since you aren't just a predator like we are, you probably have some sympathy for the prey that you can become."

She was baiting me; I could feel it.

"No, I just don't like watching things get skinned."

"How are you going to be able to handle eating a live animal then?" she asked with a smirk.

"I'm pretty sure that any animal I eat will be dead before I start eating it," I replied with a snort. "And I'll do what I have to in order to survive."

"Hopefully you'll be able to survive Werewood without your protector around," she taunted.

I rolled my eyes at her and ignored her as we ate and made the trip towards the forest. The closer we got, the more the hairs on the base of my neck stood up. The forest was dark, even the bark of the trees was dark, and there were animals that made haunting calls inside. It was no wonder people were terrified of this place.

"You can still back out," Anastacia offered.

"I'm going back to the boundary," Maria whispered and turned around with a few of the others to go back to the Shifter side.

I waved and walked into the forest, the darkness swallowed me as soon as I entered. It took a moment, but soon my eyes adjusted and I was able to make out my surroundings, although vaguely.

Anastacia stepped in front of me and punched me in the face.

I stumbled backwards and rubbed my jaw. "I thought we had patched things up?" I asked her with a scowl.

"We will never be friends," she snapped. "You're an abomination. My parents explained everything to me. Your kind caused wars between families and friends by posing as them. I won't let you do anything like that to me or my family."

"I'm not like that," I growled at her.

"I'm not taking chances," she replied.

Carlton, Cecilia, Brent, and one of the other males I did not know walked out of the tree line to join Anastacia.

"Cecilia, you too?" I asked in disbelief.

"I didn't survive that orphanage just to be worried about some morphing chick stabbing me in the back," she whispered.

I backed away slowly, but they continued advancing on me. "I haven't done anything. You can't just beat me for a crime I haven't committed."

"Oh, we aren't beating you, we're taking you out before you have the chance," Anastacia explained.

They were going to kill me. I spun around and ran as fast as I could, jerking around trees at the last second and slamming my shoulders into them a few times. They were hot on my heels and no matter how much I weaved or how fast I ran, I could not out run them.

I tried to shift, but I was too frazzled and could not focus. I jumped over a fallen log and Anastacia tackled me from the side. I screamed in shock and tried to protect my face with my arms, but she didn't stop her attacks. I tried to get up, to hit her, kick one of them, but there were five of them and one of me. My head swam, my ears rang, and my face swelled up as they continued to beat me.

"That's enough," Cecilia snapped. "She'll be dead by morning. Let the animals finish her off so they cover our tracks. Plus, we've wandered really deep and I want to get the hell out of here."

"She's right," Anastacia agreed, panting from exerting herself. "Let's go."

If I could have cried, I would have, but my body felt like it was shutting down. I tried to sit up, but my ribs were broken in several places and I screamed in pain as I tried to move.

I lay on the ground, broken and bleeding, and listened to the sound of people who were supposed to be my friends laugh as they left me to die.

Werewood Forest loomed silently around me as I began to die. How soon until one of its predators would come and finish me off?

CHAPTER FOUR

I dreamt of a man with horns rescuing me. I didn't know what that meant, but I was certain my dreams journal wouldn't have an explanation for that dream situation. I faded in and out of consciousness and hallucinated several strange scenes. The most vivid scene was of being carried into a castle by the strange man with horns.

"WILL SHE SURVIVE?" A MAN ASKED GRUFFLY.

"Yes. Had you been an hour later, she would not, but she will survive," a soft female voice answered.

"How long until she regains full consciousness?" the man asked.

"Tomorrow morning, hopefully."

I tried to open my eyes and speak, but my words would not come out and my eyes would not open.

When my eyes finally did open, I found myself in a dark room, lying on a very soft bed.

"She awakens," the male voice I had heard before said.

"Water," I requested.

A straw was pressed to my lips and I drunk greedily.

"Not too much or you will just throw it all up."

I stopped drinking and lay my head back down on the pillow. "Thank you."

"What happened to you?" he asked.

I didn't want to talk about it so I just turned my head away and tried to stop the tears streaming down my cheeks.

"Do you have an affiliation?" he asked.

I did not respond again.

"You smell of Shifter, but I cannot tell if that is from the one who beat you or you," he told me.

They left me to die. Even Cecilia. Why? Why would they condemn me before I even had a chance? I was no threat to them. I would not have been. I even tried to make up with Anastacia.

"I'll come back after you have had some time to calm down," he told me and then left the room.

I did not want to lie in the bed any longer so I grabbed the comforter and walked around the room to inspect it. It appeared to be a bedroom, but all of the drawers were empty. At the far end of the room there was a set of thick black drapes. I pushed one aside and was momentarily blinded by the sunlight. I was definitely in a castle, the courtyard spanned out below me and many men with horns practiced fighting with weapons and hand to hand combat. Were they demons? They had said that Werewood Forest was in the Demons' territory.

Watching them fight brought back unpleasant memories of the Hall of Jackals. I let the drape fall back into place and sat down in the corner of the room, blanket bundled up around me. What was I going to do?

Sometime later the man came back and it took him a moment

to find me. His lips pressed into a thin line and he squatted down in front of me.

"Are you in pain?" he asked softly.

Emotionally. Yes. Physically. No.

"Are you hungry?" He tried.

Yes, but I didn't feel like eating.

He sighed softly and whispered, "I don't know what happened to you, but you are safe here. Okay? I promise that nothing will hurt you while you're on my lands."

As reassuring as that was, I still didn't care. Part of me felt that they should have finished me off. Perhaps it was better to let me die. Why was I so naïve as to think that they were my friends? I was an idiot. A gullible idiot.

He visited me often as did the female healer. She put an IV in my arm and hooked me up to a bag of fluids that now hung on a silver thing next to me. I did not move except to use the restroom and sometimes stayed in the restroom afterwards.

"She's not improving," the healer told him.

"I can see that."

"Perhaps it would be best to contact the Shifters and send her back to them," she suggested.

Back? No, if I went back they would kill me for sure.

"Alright, I'll contact…"

"No!" I gasped and tried to stand up, but my legs wouldn't hold me up. I fell forward onto my hands. "Please, don't. I can't go back. Never!" I cried. My body began shaking and tears threatened to break lose.

The man squatted down next to me and helped me sit up against the wall again. "Okay, calm down. I won't contact them."

"If you don't eat you'll die," the healer told me.

I looked down at my pale arms and whispered, "Maybe I should."

The man gripped my chin roughly and lifted my face. "I saved you. You will eat and you will live. Do you understand?"

He was terrifying in that moment and yet I knew he was doing it to try to keep me alive.

"Okay," I conceded.

"Sanora, bathe and dress her," the man ordered and released my chin.

"Yes, sir."

He left and she removed the IV. I didn't want to let her see me naked, but since she had healed me, I was certain she already had. She drew a bath and scrubbed me thoroughly. I had not realized how filthy I was and as the bath water clouded with mud, I felt bad about the sheets I had been sleeping in.

"Your clothes were ruined," Sanora told me, "But I found some that should fit you."

She had to help me dress and then together we stripped the bed for cleaning. I could tell she wanted to ask me questions, but she thankfully did not.

"I'll go let him know that you are ready."

"Ready for what?" I asked nervously.

She shrugged. "I don't know."

I found a spare blanket in one of the drawers and wrapped it around myself, sitting back in the corner of the room I had favored so much these past few days. How long had it been since they left me for dead?

"You need to get some fresh air," he told me when he returned.

"I don't...people..." I tried to explain, but I was gasping for breath. I was having a panic attack. I hadn't had one since I was in junior high.

He picked me up, blanket and all, and carried me in his arms out of the room. "Deep breaths," he whispered.

I obeyed, trying to calm my now racing heart. We walked down a long hallway, down a flight of stairs, and then out into the courtyard I had looked at before. It was empty, thank goodness, and there was a tree to one side that I had not noticed before. He set me down so that my back leaned against the tree and then sat down beside me.

"I come out here to think," he told me. "It's often a very busy place, but when everyone is gone, it is incredibly relaxing."

I breathed in the cool, crisp air and my heart returned to its normal rhythm. I expected him to probe me for answers, but he simply sat next to me in silence.

I should have thanked him, but lost my voice as he picked me up and took me back to my room when the sun set. Sanora brought me food and once she left, I ate it. He returned the following day and took me outside again. Still he did not ask me questions and I still did not speak to him or offer any answers. On the fourth day, just as the sun began to set I finally opened my mouth.

"Thank you," I whispered.

"She speaks," he gasped in fake shock.

"Who are you?" I asked softly.

"My name is Zydon, I am the ruler of the Enki'l. Some call us Demons."

Demons, I was right. They didn't seem evil though. Perhaps our version of demons and these were not the same. Wait, he had used another name. Enki'l.

"I'm Celwyn," I whispered in response.

"That is a lovely name," he complimented. I didn't have anything else I wanted to say, but he finally asked the dreaded question. "Where are you from?"

"My family is from a faraway place and after the magic returned, we moved to the island. My father is a Shifter and he moved us to be with the Shifters at the Hall of Jackals."

"You are a Shifter," he whispered.

"I can't go back," I whispered. "They will finish what they failed to complete."

"Who hurt you? Was it Merle or Mauricio?"

I shook my head. "Other new Shifters."

"Why did they attack you?"

"I'm not like them," I whispered and then in an even softer voice added, "I'm a Therianthrope."

He growled softly and stood up, pacing in front of me. "Those stupid idiots."

"I didn't even do anything," I whispered as the tears finally spilled over. "They said they couldn't take the chance that I might betray them. I would never have betrayed them."

"Who is your father?" he asked.

"Tyren of the Werewolves."

"Tyren? I'm surprised he survived all these years away from Olansia," he said. "I'm even more surprised he would bring you here. He knows how set in their ways the older ones are."

"He thought I would be safe because Chuck, Charles, regained his place as Second and placed me under his protection," I explained.

"Charles has returned as well? This day is full of surprises."

"Are you going to kill me?" I asked nervously. I probably should not have told him what I was.

He squatted down in front of me and looked at me very seriously. Now that I was really looking at him, he was handsome. His face was very humanlike and the horns actually made him more attractive, in some weird way. "I don't care what you are. I saved you and placed you under my protection. I will not renege on that."

"What am I going to do?" I asked as new tears flowed. These tears were out of fear of the unknown future before me.

"You are going to start by eating with me," he said and picked me up. "We will take things one step at a time and you can decide what you wish to do when you are ready."

"Why? Why would you do this for me? You don't know me. You might be safer killing me, like they said."

He smiled and it made my stomach quiver with butterflies. "I'm very certain that you pose no threat to me, especially in your current condition. As to why I'm doing this, I found you in the forest, beaten and broken, and though I could have left you, some part of me felt that you deserved a chance to live. Some part of me felt a connection to you."

I had no response to his words, so I dropped my head to his chest and let him take me into the castle and to a room with a long wooden table. He set me in a chair on one end and then took the seat at the other end. Several Enki'ls came out without being called and began serving us food. There was salad, bread, meat, and a potato dish of some kind. I ate everything that they put on my plate and drank four full cups of water. Zydon watched me, but never spoke. Who was this Enki'l? He was obviously someone important and he said this was his land. Was he a King or the Alpha?

"Thank you, dinner was wonderful," I said with a smile. Possibly the first smile I had worn in over a week.

"I'm glad that you liked it. Would you like to meet the others?"

"I'm still tired," I said quickly, "I'd like to return to my room." I tried to stand up, but as soon as I took my first step, I fell forward. Zydon rushed around the table and caught me around the chest, my face narrowly missing smacking into the ground.

"Let me take you back," he offered. "Your muscles haven't been used and are weak."

"That's all I am," I whispered softly. "Weak."

"You don't have to be. You could become strong," he said as he picked me up. "Even the strongest person started as a baby, dependent on their family to survive."

"I've lost my family," I whispered.

"I can fill in," he offered. "If you'd like me to, I can help you learn to be stronger and more powerful."

"You've already done so much..."

"Tomorrow, we will start. Okay?" he whispered. We were already at my room and he set me down on my bed, which was freshly made.

"Okay," I agreed. I wanted to be stronger. I needed to be stronger. All those years of being the alpha female as a human meant nothing. Here, I was a weakling. It was time that I worked to change that.

WHEN HE ARRIVED THE NEXT MORNING, I WAS UP AND DRESSED already. He put his arm around my waist and we slowly walked down the hallway while I used my own legs. Halfway down the hallway my legs began shaking and they gave out from under me. He supported my weight and lifted me up into his arms.

"That's a good start," he said.

"I didn't even make it down the hallway," I argued.

"It's farther than you made it yesterday."

We ate breakfast alone and then he took me into a lower level of the castle, one that was deep underground. The stone turned into tile and a huge pool took up the entire level below.

"Your muscles are too weak for us to accomplish much. So, we will use water to help speed your recovery," he explained.

He set me down at the edge of the pool and I dipped my toe into the water. It was warm and smelled minty.

"This is a healing pool, the water comes from a hot spring far below here," he explained as he took off his shirt.

I looked away before he caught me ogling him and his incredible amount of muscles. I worried that he would make me strip, but after sliding into the water himself, he lifted me by my waist into the water and swam out away from the edge. I gripped his shoulders and he smiled, amused.

"Keep your grip on my shoulders and slowly kick your legs," he instructed me.

The water provided resistance as I moved my legs and the healing qualities began working, tingling all over. He swam backwards, lazily, while I kicked my feet and held onto him. His smile was warm and kind and I realized that I had allowed myself to be vulnerable to this man that I did not know. This demon that I did not know.

Should I trust him? He seemed trustworthy, but what did I really know about him.

"What's wrong?" he asked.

I had stopped kicking my legs. "I, uh, I realized that I don't know anything about you."

He continued his lazy swimming and said, "Well, I suppose during the time that you weren't talking, I could have been talking to you. I just figured you wanted silence."

"I did."

"Well, what do you want to know?" he asked.

"Everything," I said.

He laughed and said, "That would take a very long time."

"Okay, well tell me whatever you want to tell me," I said with a shrug.

"Well you know my name and you know I'm an Enki'l. I didn't tell you that I am the leader of the Enki'ls."

"Like the Alpha?" I asked.

"More like the King," he corrected.

"Oh," I whispered in shock.

"I built this castle with the other Enki'ls who reside here. It was the cost to live here."

"To live here they had to help build it?" I asked.

He nodded.

"What if new Enki'l come and want to stay here?" I asked.

"There are other things they can do to earn their keep. Some patrol our territory and some I send on missions. Others are servants here."

"Is there a female leader, a Queen?" I asked.

He shook his head. "Unlike the Shifters, I do not have a need for a female counter."

"So, you're not married or mated?" I asked and focused really hard on looking at the water between us.

"No," he said softly. "I've not found my mate. It may be that I do not have one."

"You believe in soul mates?" I asked in shock.

"You find that strange?" he asked me.

"We don't believe in soul mates where I am from," I said.

"What do you believe in?" he asked.

I stopped kicking my legs and let him keep me afloat. "Not much," I replied in shock. I had never really thought about it before. We didn't go to church or have beliefs in nature spirits or any of the mainstream religions. I didn't believe in soul mates or true love. I didn't really believe in anything.

"I know it can be hard to find things to believe in and must be even harder now that your world has been turned upside down," he said. "Perhaps you need to find something to believe in."

I didn't find that likely, but didn't want to say that to him. What could there be for me to believe in here on this crazy island?

"Are you ready to stop?" he asked.

"No, I can do more," I replied quickly.

"Do you want to try swimming on your own?" he suggested.

"Okay," I agreed.

He swam to the shallow end and I let go of his shoulders. I had not been swimming for a long time, but I found my rhythm after a few strokes and began swimming laps. After just four laps I was exhausted.

I tried to do another lap, but Zydon grabbed me as I struggled to swim the last half of the pool. "That's enough for today," he said and carried me out of the pool.

"I'm sorry. I want to do more. I just…"

"A soldier does what he can. If he is at his limit, he cannot do more or he may hurt himself and then become useless," he said.

"Is that a quote from somewhere?" I asked him.

"No, that's what I tell my soldiers when we are preparing for battle," he explained.

I laughed softly and said, "Well I'm hardly a soldier."

"No, but you will be."

"You're going to make me a soldier?" I asked in shock.

He smiled. "I plan to help you be the best that you can be."

"Uh…" I replied with my genius brain.

He stopped at a room above the pool and set me down on a bench. There were three areas covered by white curtains. "There are showers here," he offered.

"I'll wait until I get to the room," I said, not wanting to admit that I probably could not hold myself up to shower or wash my hair by myself with how drained I was.

"Okay, then give me just a few minutes," he said and walked behind one of the curtains. Water turned on a bit later.

I chewed on my lip as I struggled to keep my mind out of the gutter, or shower at the moment. A few minutes later he came out in new clothes. I wasn't sure where he had kept them, but since this was his castle, it made sense that he had clothes stored in places like this.

"How are you feeling?" he asked.

"Tired, but I feel a lot better," I admitted.

"Tomorrow you will feel even better," he assured me. "The springs always take a night to work."

"Do you know Merle?" I asked him.

He picked me up and began climbing the stairs to the upper levels. Had he been human, his strength would not have been enough to continue carrying me. As he was, he lifted me with no more struggle than I would a jug of milk.

"I do, but we haven't had much contact the last few decades."

"If he finds out I am alive, will he force me to return?" It was something I was worried about. If he forced me to return and discovered that I had been living at Zydon's, would he assume I was a traitor and kill me? Was he planning to kill me anyways?

"He might," he agreed.

"Is there a way to keep him from finding out?" I asked him hopefully.

"I have not sent them contact and my people know to leave such matters to me. If a visitor saw you, they might report back to them, but we have not had visitors in a very long time," he assured me.

I nodded my head and then leaned it against his shoulder. I felt so comfortable with him and safe. It reminded me of how Mom's paranormal romance books described the main male character. Could this be the start of my own paranormal romance story?

I laughed softly at my ridiculousness and Zydon looked own at me quizzically. I turned my face down since I did not want to even begin to try to explain what I had just been thinking.

Instead of just leaving me in my room, he had one of the female Enki'l help me bathe and change and then he sat on the floor with me to play a card game. The cards had strange symbols and I realized that it was very odd for us to be able to communicate so well.

"Why do you speak English like I do?" I asked him.

"I am not speaking English right now," he corrected me. "I put a spell on you that allows everything you hear to be translated into your native tongue and I have the same spell on myself, as does every being on Olansia."

"Why didn't I have it placed on me when I landed?" I asked.

"You did, but almost dying caused it to break," he answered. His fists clenched and he exhaled loudly before loosing them.

"Why can't I read the symbols then?" I asked.

"The spell is only on your ears, for hearing. For the game, you'll just have to learn as we go."

"Can you teach me your language?" I asked.

He blinked in silence a few times and asked, "You want to learn my language?"

I nodded. "If it's not too much trouble."

"No, but learning the language of Enki'ls won't be useful except for with other Enki'ls."

"I'm in Enki'l territory," I reminded him, "And I don't know how soon I will be leaving." If ever.

"Very well. I will teach you. Tonight, let's just play some games. I'm sure that you will be able to figure it out as we go."

He was right, the game he taught me was very similar to Go Fish. We played well into the night and we laughed and teased each other. When we began yawning uncontrollably, he packed up the cards and lifted me into my bed. "Good night, Celwyn."

"Good night, Zydon."

He pressed a light kiss to my forehead before leaving and I fell asleep with the warmth of his kiss still there.

"Celwyn," Chuck whispered. "Where are you? I know you're alive. Your Dad can feel you. Where are you girl?"

"Chuck?" I whispered in shock. I tried to open my eyes, but couldn't. "What?"

"Stop struggling. This type of communication is very difficult. Just tell me where you are so I can come get you," he ordered me.

"No," I gasped. "No. I am never coming back."

"What? Celwyn, you're speaking nonsense. You need to come back."

"No!" I screamed and tried to wake up. "No!"

"Celwyn!" he yelled. "Where are you? What happened?"

"They'll kill me!" I screamed at him. "No!"

"Celwyn!"

"Celwyn!" Zydon yelled as he shook my shoulders.

My eyes opened and I gasped in shock, my heart hammered against my rib cage.

Zydon cradled me in his lap and hugged me against his chest. "It's alright. I've got you."

I sniffled and clung to him like a pathetic child. "I don't want to go back. I don't want to go."

"You're not going anywhere," he promised me. "You're safe. I won't let anyone hurt you."

"They'll kill me," I sobbed.

"No one is going to kill you," he swore. "I won't let anyone take you away."

My chest ached and my breathing became erratic. I tried to calm myself down, but panic attacks don't listen to anyone. Zydon rocked me and said reassuring things, but it wasn't helping. He wrapped me up in my blanket and set me in the corner on the floor where I had been the first week. He started to back away, but I grabbed his hand and he sat down beside me. I closed my eyes and took deep breaths.

I was safe.

Zydon was here.

Chuck did not know where I was.

No one was coming to get me.

I was safe.

Zydon was here.

Zydon would not let them take me.

Eventually the panic lessened enough for me to doze and then Zydon pulled me down so my head lay in his lap. He stroked my hair softly and sang a song I did not know. The pressure eased slowly and thankfully released, allowing me to fall asleep.

"I hate to wake you, but my legs have fallen asleep," Zydon whispered in my ear.

I sat up and he stretched with a groan. "I'm sorry," I whispered and stumbled towards my bed.

He covered me up and kissed my forehead. "Go back to sleep, Celwyn."

I didn't think I would be able to, but I slept more. When I finally did wake, it was past midday. Since Zydon did not come for me, I dressed and headed down the hallway. The walk took forever and on several occasions, I swore the hallway lengthened itself. With one hand on the wall, I took one step at a time until I made it to the dining room. Zydon was not there either. A female Enki'l brought me out food and drink and then disappeared.

I finished my food and stared at his empty seat. Maybe he was still sleeping. Another glass of water was brought to me and I finished it before heading out to the courtyard. The soldiers were practicing sword fighting and Zydon was in the center of them, practicing as well. I sat on the stairs that led down to the courtyard and leaned against a raised planter on the side to watch them.

They all moved with such precision and experience, there was no doubt that they were seasoned soldiers. Zydon sparred with his soldiers, three of them attacked him hand to hand and he blocked their attacks. At the end of their sparring, everyone smiled and patted each other on the back. There was obvious comradery amongst them and it was clear that Zydon was loved by his men. Could I have had an experience like this with the Shifters had I not been a Therian? Could Anastacia and I have been friends who sparred together and smiled afterwards?

He noticed me as he finished a conversation with one of the soldiers and walked over to me with a smile. "Hello, Sunshine."

"I'm sorry I woke you last night," I apologized.

He took my hand and pulled me into a standing position. "You woke the entire castle," he informed me.

I blushed and looked down at my feet. "Oh."

"So, this is the girl who woke us last night?" one of the soldiers asked. He had dark brown hair, bronze skin, and a scar on the edge of his mouth. His horns were shorter than Zydon's and more twisted.

"Celwyn, this is my Second, Lars," Zydon introduced, "Lars, this is Celwyn. The banshee herself."

He bowed slightly and said, "It's nice to meet you, Celwyn."

"Sorry about last night," I apologized again.

"We all have nightmares occasionally," he said with a nonchalant shrug.

If only it had just been a nightmare.

"It wasn't a nightmare, was it?" Zydon asked.

I shook my head as I stared at the stone ground. It was well worn with age. How long had this castle been standing?

"What was it?" Lars asked.

"Charles was trying to contact me. He said they knew I was alive because Dad can feel me. He said I needed to come back."

"Did you tell him where you were?" Zydon asked.

I shook my head.

"That explains why she was screaming 'no' and sounded so scared," Lars whispered and there was no irritation or judgment in his tone.

"Are you ready for today's lesson?" Zydon asked, changing the subject.

I nodded and followed him to the center of the courtyard. There were still several soldiers around, many stayed to watch when they noticed me.

"Punch me," Zydon ordered me.

"Uh," I said and looked at him.

"Come on, punch me in the stomach as hard as you can," he said.

I obeyed and he showed me a better way to punch.

"Again."

His abs were so hard, that they hurt my knuckles.

"Punch him," he said and set a dummy made of straw in front of me. "Keep your legs shoulder width and take even breaths."

It wasn't long before I was exhausted again, but I smiled like a moron at the little improvement I had made on my punching technique.

"Good," he praised as he lifted me in his arms and carried me into the castle. "Now, let's eat some lunch."

I thought it would just be the two of us, but the soldiers followed us inside the castle. Zydon carried me into a different room, one I had not been in before, where many tables were set up. It reminded me of a high school cafeteria except the tables were solid wood. The soldiers took seats at the tables and Zydon set me on a bench next to Lars.

"So, what can you tell us about yourself?" Lars asked.

The soldiers were a bit too quiet, trying to appear distracted, yet I knew they were listening to our conversation.

"I'm twenty-two years old," I said, "I lived in the country of the United States of America, in a state called California with my mom and dad. My dad and his best friend, who I called my uncle even though there was no blood relation, were always wary of the Government and I never knew why, until now."

Zydon had taken a seat across the table from me and his eyes were wide. "You lived out there? What's it like? How has it changed?"

"I'm not an expert on anything," I said right away, "And Dad or Charles would be better able to tell you things, but I can tell you some. Technology has improved drastically since you were last in this dimension. We have devices that let us communicate to each other no matter where in the world we are. We can take a picture, a digital painting, and send it around the world. We have machines that will send electricity to a heart if it has stopped to restart it. We use cars to drive around, boats to drive on the sea, and airplanes to fly in the air. The human population has increased a lot, I don't know specific numbers from when you were here last, but there are billions of people on the planet now."

The soldiers murmured to each other in shock and I knew many had questions. Sadly, I could not answer them.

"I'm sorry, I don't have a lot of knowledge to be able to explain things to you," I replied gloomily.

"You said you didn't know why they were wary of the Government until now," Lars asked, "What happened?"

"When magic returned, a lot of people began using their powers for stealing, killing, or just causing mayhem. The Government decided it was best to round up everyone with powers. They claimed they were going to determine who was a threat or not, but we're pretty certain that they were either going to experiment on people or kill them. Possibly both."

"Did they catch you?" Lars asked.

I shook my head. "They almost did, but Dad was able to get us out and they were able to get us to Olansia using their magic."

"Why didn't you know before what you were?" one of the soldiers asked.

"Dad used to say he was a werewolf all the time, but it was said jokingly and only after he would do something odd. Like, he always smelled the top of Mom's head. And he was super protective and possessive of her when they first started dating. We thought he was joking, but clearly he wasn't. Without magic I had no way of knowing I was a Shifter."

Servants brought out food and drink for everyone and conversation shifted away from me. I ate my food and then watched those around me. There were no female soldiers, in fact, the only females I had seen were a few servants and the healers.

"Where are your females?" I asked Lars.

"There are very few female Enki'l," he explained, "Most of the Enki'l born are male."

"Is that why there are so few of you?" I asked.

He smirked. "There are various reasons, but yes that is a major reason."

"Were you married to someone, before coming here?" a soldier on my left asked.

I shook my head. "No, I've never been married or mated. Where I came from, men were, um, not as strong and I found it difficult to find someone."

"Not as strong? Before magic you would have had equal strength, right?" Lars asked.

"Yes, I don't really mean just physically strong. A lot of guys just weren't very masculine, which isn't a bad thing. I just prefer masculine men."

"Being around Tyren and Charles would have preconditioned you to seek out similar qualities in a mate," Lars said. "It makes sense that if there were no other males who exhibited strong masculine characteristics that you would not find them appealing."

I guess that did make sense. I wasn't consciously comparing the guys I knew to them, but when I did compare them, it was a sadly large gap between them. I knew some masculine men, but a lot of them were egotistical or just too cocky for my liking. Maybe I was damned if I did and damned if I didn't when it came to men. I liked them masculine, but found most masculine men too egotistical. Maybe I should go rent an apartment and buy a horde of cats to live out the rest of my spinster life.

"I think you'll find your choices on Olansia are much broader," Lars said. "Men don't survive without being masculine, unless they live South with the mages."

"Good to know that I will have more options," I replied with a smile despite the pit of dread in my stomach that I might not live out the year or month with the way things were going for me here.

"Are you finished eating?" Zydon asked me.

I had almost forgotten he was there, he had been so quiet. I couldn't completely forget he was there because he had a presence, an aura about him that kept a part of me always aware he was nearby.

"Yes."

"Then we should get to your second lesson of the day," he said. He stood up and I followed his lead.

"Thank you, for allowing me to eat with you," I thanked Lars and the others.

"You are always welcome to join us," Lars invited.

I smiled in return and then followed Zydon out of the room. When the door shut behind us, he picked me up and headed towards the stairway that led to the pool below ground.

"I think I can walk down there," I offered.

"I'd rather you conserve your strength for exercising in the pool," he explained.

"The others," I began and fiddled with the edge of his shirt sleeve, "They all seem nice."

"They are a good group," he agreed, "And they've been asking to meet you since I brought you here."

"Why?"

"Lars especially wanted to help you in any way that he could, but I thought it best that you have limited contact in the beginning. We have been isolated for a while and to find you like we did, I believe has lit a fire beneath them that had long since cooled."

"I'm not really following," I admitted.

He set me on the edge of the pool and removed his shirt again. This time, he also removed his pants, but had on a pair of shorts, though my heart, and other parts, warmed as he removed his pants. And I had to admit I was a tad disappointed. Stupid hormones.

He climbed into the water and lifted me with him. "We used to be the protectors of humans," he explained to me. "We were the ones who would fight the other beings who threatened the humans. When we left this dimension, the humans who still lived on Olansia moved down with the mages and shunned us. Without the humans to protect, we had no real directive."

"How do I come into this?" I asked since I wasn't sure what he was getting at.

"I believe finding you, near death, reminded them how fragile humans are and that there are people out there who need our protection."

"I'm glad my weakness could be of service," I muttered bitterly and swam away from him to do my laps.

"Celwyn, that's not what I meant by what I said," he replied immediately.

I ignored him and swam back and forth across the pool. I was able to swim twice as many laps despite having trained earlier in the same day. It would have made me happier had he not just reminded me of how pathetic I was.

He had moved off to the side and stayed silent as I swam, but when I stopped and leaned against the wall, he swam to me and picked me up. I wanted to tell him to leave me alone, but there was no way I could make it up the stairs.

"I'm sorry if I upset you," he spoke softly as we ascended the stairs.

"It's not your fault that I'm useless," I whispered sadly. "Perhaps I should leave and let Chuck pick me up."

"You are free to leave whenever you want," he told me, "but if you wish to stay here, I will protect you and help you get stronger."

"What if I can't get strong enough?" I asked. "What if I'm never able to survive out there?"

"Then you'll stay here," he said nonchalantly.

"I'm a burden to whoever I'm with," I whispered.

We were in front of my room and he jerked to a stop, just out of reach of the door. "That's enough," he ordered in an angry tone. "Stop feeling sorry for yourself. If you want to change, then do it. You can spend tonight wallowing, but tomorrow either you work on changing or you don't, but I do not want to hear you feeling sorry for yourself after tonight. Do you understand? I will do whatever I can to help you. Okay?"

I nodded and he kissed my forehead. "Tomorrow is a new day. Tomorrow is a new start."

CHAPTER FIVE

Zydon found me the next morning in the courtyard with Lars practicing hand to hand combat. He sat against the tree and closed his eyes. Lars showed me a few more moves and then called an end to our morning so we could go eat breakfast. I followed Lars inside, well aware of the fact that Zydon had not followed us.

"Are you two fighting?" Lars asked softly once we were inside.

"No," I answered truthfully. "I'm just trying to focus. Plus, I'm sure he has things he has been putting aside to deal with me." It really did not make sense that he had spent so much time on me himself when he could have easily assigned Lars or one of the others.

"Well, I haven't a thing to do, so you're welcome to pester me whenever you want," he offered.

We sat at one of the tables and I drank three glasses of water before the food was even brought out.

"Have you been to the armory yet?" one of the Enki'l at the table asked me. He was massive, bulky like a bodybuilder, with green eyes and had short, but very thick horns.

"No," I answered.

"I'll take you after we finish eating," he said.

"I'm sorry, what's your name?" I asked sheepishly.

"No, I'm sorry. I didn't introduce myself yet. I'm Jeff."

Jeff?

"It's nice to meet you. And why are we going to the armory?"

Lars laughed. "Jeff is our weapons master. He is in charge of the armory and firmly believes that everyone should walk around with at least one weapon on their bodies at all times, even in the shower."

"Definitely in the shower," Jeff said.

"I've never handled swords or knives. I have shot guns a few times, but my parents were into it more than I was," I explained.

"That will just be one more thing we work on teaching you," Jeff said nonchalantly.

"I don't know how long I'll be here. I feel like I'll wear out my welcome long before I am able to master anything," I admitted to them and looked towards the door. Zydon hadn't come in yet.

"You have a place here as long as you want one," Lars told me.

"What if I want to stay here forever?" I asked with a smirk.

Lars smiled. "Then we will have a long time to get to know each other."

I laughed loudly, feeling my worries slowly leaking away. Maybe I could like it here. Maybe I could learn to live here. I would have to find some way to make myself useful. Perhaps after some more training, I could check out the servants' chores and see if I could be used in laundry or housekeeping somewhere.

Food was served and I found that my appetite had increased dramatically. I ate more than I had ever eaten before. I would have felt embarrassed except everyone around me was eating twice as much as I was. Zydon came in when I had finished eating. I left without speaking to him and followed Jeff out past the courtyard and to a small door I had not noticed before. The room we entered was filled with every type of medieval weapon one could imagine and more. The swords and daggers were beautiful and I picked up one at the far end of the room.

"For your size, I'm not sure what sword you will be best equipped to handle," Jeff said. "We can have you try a few out and then decide which one of that style you want afterwards."

"Or, we can make you a new one to your specifications," Zydon said from behind me.

I almost dropped the sword I was holding, shocked to hear him since I had not noticed him enter the room.

"I don't think new ones will be necessary," I said and put the sword back in the rack. "There are plenty here for me to choose from."

He picked up a wrist guard, picked up my hand, and slid it into place. "Jeff, I'll help her pick out her items."

Jeff bowed his head and left the armory.

"I'm sure you have other things that require your attention," I told him while facing the swords. "You don't need to waste any more time on me. Lars and the others have offered to help me."

"What if I want to spend time with you?" he asked. "Would you prefer to work with them instead of me?"

"If you want to help me, I wouldn't turn you down," I said. "You're the leader after all."

"I heard that you were considering staying here," he whispered from very close to me.

"I was discussing my options," I lied, "And they said I was welcome to stay here. Of course, if I thought that decision was likely, I would talk to you first and get your approval. That decision is far off anyway. I haven't been here more than a month yet."

"They like you," he said, "They are drawn to you, like I am. Something about you is magnetic."

"I think that's a compliment," I said with a soft laugh.

He put the other wrist guard on. "There are many options for armor. We don't have armor often in your size, but I can talk to our armorer about making you some."

"I don't need special armor or new things. I'm not a soldier and I can make do with what is here," I assured him.

"Would you eat dinner with me tonight?" he asked, "After you have finished your trainings?"

"Haven't we been eating meals together?" I asked with a smirk.

"Yes, but this time I am requesting your presence."

"Okay," I agreed.

He picked up a sword and held it out to me. "This will be a good sword for you to learn with," he said. I took the sword and then he kissed my cheek. "See you later."

I stood in disbelief in the armory and held the sword he had given me. I was going on a date with the King of Enki'ls. My life had changed so much in two months. Maybe I was in a coma and this was a complete dream. If so, my dreams were strange and wonderful.

"Celwyn!" Chuck yelled in my head.

I screamed in shock and dropped the sword as I clutched my head. Jeff rushed in and picked me up from the floor where I had fallen. He rushed me from the armory to Zydon who hadn't gotten far from the entrance.

Zydon grabbed my head with his hands and his scent surrounded me. Chuck's presence disappeared and I gasped in relief.

"Thank you," I whispered as I gasped for breath.

"He's trying very hard to contact you," Zydon informed me. "That type of communication would have hurt him as much as it hurt you."

"What should I do?" I asked. "I don't want to go back. Can he track me? Or could my Dad?" I asked nervously.

"Yes, but you are guarded a bit here thanks to my shields," he explained, "So, they cannot exactly pinpoint you."

"What if they somehow find me? What if they track me here or at least nearby and come here?"

He hugged me and whispered, "I'll protect you. I won't let them take you anywhere that you do not want to go."

"What if they try to fight?" I asked him. "You shouldn't get in a fight for something that does not concern you."

"It concerns us plenty," Lars said.

"My sword," I whispered, "I dropped it in the armory."

"We'll get it later. Now you need to rest," Zydon ordered me. He carried me to my room and set me on my bed.

"Is there a way you can keep him from contacting me?" I asked hopefully.

"Yes," he said and dragged out the s. "But it's not an option currently."

"Why not?" I asked sadly. If there was a way to keep him from contacting me, that would be the best option.

He sighed softly. "It's a permanent change that would cause a lot of consequences you most likely would not enjoy."

Why couldn't he just give me a straight answer?

"If you don't want to do it, you could just say that," I muttered and then kicked off my shoes.

"There are other options," he said.

"Like what? Meeting him somewhere? Or communicating with him outside of the castle?" I asked.

He nodded. "Yes. We could take you to the Werewood Forest and you could contact him from there to let him know that you are not returning to the Hall or the Pack."

"What if he orders me to return? Does he have power to make me do what he says?" Mom had read a few books like that, where someone could not withstand an Alpha's order.

"No, he does not have that power," he told me.

"I should probably just leave," I admitted sadly.

"Leave?" he asked.

"Chuck will keep trying to contact me and I'll be putting you at risk, so I should most likely leave. When they find me, I'm not likely to be allowed to live. Even if Chuck brought me back, the others would find some way again to try to murder me. I would be on the run for the rest of my life."

"You could go to the mages and ask them for protection," he suggested.

"And how likely do you think the mages will trust a Therianthrope?" I asked with a scowl.

"True."

"Why are you trusting me?" I asked him.

"Why are you trusting me?" he asked back.

"You saved my life," I reminded him, "If you'd wanted me dead, you would have left me in the forest."

"What if I'm planning to use you?" he asked.

"For what? Killing me wouldn't start a war with anyone. Returning me wouldn't do anything. Keeping me won't result in much and I'm pretty certain you don't care about money so ransom has no meaning for you."

He smiled. "Very perceptive."

"I'm not completely useless," I whispered. "Soon, I'll be even more useful."

"I do not doubt that for a moment," he responded.

"Can I..." I stopped and chewed on my lip.

"Can you what?" he asked.

"Can I touch your horns?" I asked quickly, my words tumbling over each other. I had wanted to ask for a while, but thought it would be rude.

He chuckled and said, "I wondered how long it would take you to ask." He tilted his head sideways and said, "Go on."

Timidly, I reached up and touched my fingertip to his black, curved horn. It was hard, of course, but surprisingly warm. I ran my fingertip over a couple ridges and then dropped my hand to my lap, embarrassed.

"Thanks."

"You're welcome to touch them anytime you want," he teased.

"Thank you, for everything," I said sincerely.

He smiled and said, "You're welcome."

"Will you promise me something?" I requested.

"What?" he asked.

"Will you promise me that if they threaten war or try to fight you in regards to me, that you will back down?"

He looked at me for a long moment in silence and then turned and headed towards the door. "No, I cannot promise you that."

"Why not?" I called out to him and stood up off the bed.

He stopped with his hand on the door handle and said, "I'm an Alpha. My job is to protect my people and those under my protection. I am also an Enki'l. Our job is to protect humanity from the supernatural when they step out of line. It goes against everything in me to not protect you."

"I'm not human," I reminded him.

"You are human. Shifters are essentially humans."

"Please, I do not want you to..."

"I'm sorry. I can't promise you that," he said and then left.

THE NEXT MORNING ZYDON WOKE ME JUST AFTER THE SUN HAD risen and asked me to meet him in the courtyard. I was incredibly nervous because he had not given me any indication as to what we were doing. Was it training? Wouldn't he have told me if we were training?

Lars, Jeff, and Zydon were standing together in the courtyard and Zydon held the reins of two horses. The horses were coal black from the tips of their ears all the way to the tips of their hooves. Even their eyes appeared black.

Approaching hesitantly, I stopped a distance from the trio and the intimidating horses.

Zydon looked at Lars and Jeff. "Lars will be in command while I'm gone. Jeff, you keep the rest from following us."

"Why can't one of us come?" Lars asked.

"Because we need someone to come rescue us if we get in trouble," Zydon answered with a smile.

"Celwyn, are you ready to go?" he asked softly.

"Where are we going?" I asked nervously.

He smiled. "Do you trust me?"

"Of course," I answered immediately.

After putting the reins over the horses' heads, he helped me up into the saddle of one, mounted his horse, and then made a noise with his tongue that had the horses walking towards the draw bridge.

"Did you sleep well?" Zydon asked.

"Yes. How about you?"

"Well, since there wasn't a banshee screaming early in the morning, I slept very well," he teased.

I stuck my tongue out at him and then turned away. He laughed softly and despite my efforts, a smile spread across my lips. The draw bridge lowered and the horses ambled across it. The land around the castle was a tall grass that came up to the horses' knees and made a gentle swishing sound as we moved through it. Birds flew past overhead, some towards the forest and others landed in the grass, chirping to unseen family. I was wearing one of Zydon's cloaks, but I still felt cold.

"It's beautiful here," I said and felt myself finally relaxing for the first time since magic had returned.

"Most find it rather boring scenery," he responded.

"If you lived in a city where everything was concrete and nature only existed in areas that we permitted it to, you would find this a breath of fresh air, literally," I told him.

"What is concrete?" he inquired.

"Crushed up rock that is mixed with something to make a hard structure that is very hard to break," I tried to explain.

"It's a building material?" he guessed.

I nodded. "Yes. It is also used for sidewalks, a level surface for us to walk on instead of dirt and rocks."

"Is it used for roads as well?"

I shook my head. "They use something that is like concrete mixed with tar. I am not exactly sure what it is, but that's the best description I can think of that you would understand."

"It sounds like an interesting place," he admitted.

"Perhaps someday you can visit it," I suggested.

"Would you be my guide?" he asked.

"If I'm alive still," I muttered and looked down at my wrist guards.

Zydon moved his horse closer to mine and reached out, setting his hand on top of the one that held the reins. "Pessimism does not suit you. I will do everything within my power to keep you alive. Will you promise me something?"

"What?"

"Will you promise me to try your hardest to stay alive so that when things have calmed down enough for us to safely travel, you can be my guide to the world you come from?"

I blushed slightly and said. "If you're not sick of me yet, I will happily show you around the world I come from."

He squeezed my hand and then released me to move his horse away again. He took a path to the right and we headed towards the Werewood Forest.

"Where are we going?" I asked.

"I thought that you might enjoy a chance to escape the castle," he told me.

Definitely, but being able to spend time alone with him was a definite bonus.

The grasses turned into a beautiful flower patch with flowers similar to hibiscus ranging in colors from royal blue to lavender to even hot pink. Zydon fell over sideways, with only his leg in the stirrup on the right side and his hand on the horn keeping him in the saddle. I gasped in shock, but he corrected himself after a moment and then held out a royal blue flower towards me.

I exhaled in relief. "You startled me. I thought you had fallen out of the saddle."

He smirked and said. "I would hope you have a little more faith in me than to expect me to fall so easily."

I rolled my eyes at him and then sat still as a stone as he moved his horse closer and tucked the flower above my ear.

"It matches your eyes," he told me.

My eyes were nowhere near as beautiful as the flower's color, but I accepted the compliment. "Thank you. It is beautiful."

We entered the forest and I gulped nervously. We had traveled for a long time, the castle long behind us and the Werewood Forest around us, thick and dark. My mouth was dry and my hands were clammy. He really hadn't said much to me so far this morning, but I tried not to let it bother me. I really had to start finding things to do around the castle when we got back.

Deep within the Werewood Forest, we traveled down a trail that led to a small creek and on the opposite bank was a gorgeous weeping cherry tree in full bloom with pink blossoms littering the ground around it.

"Oh," I whispered in shock. It was the most beautiful thing I had ever seen in my life. A slice of beauty in an otherwise dark place.

We stopped the horses, dismounted, and tied them to the ground with long leads so they could drink from the stream if they wanted. Zydon hopped across the creek and held out his hand to me. "Come on," he coaxed.

I set my hand in his and jumped across, but lost my footing and stumbled forward when I landed. My stumble put me right into his chest and he wrapped his arms around me to steady me. "Sorry," I whispered.

He tucked hair that had fallen forward behind the flower he

had put on my ear and smiled down at me. "It's been so long since I've seen a woman who blushes so often."

Despite my best wishes, I could not control my blushing. I had not even realized that I was blushing.

"It's uncontrollable," I whispered.

His fingertips skimmed the top of my cheeks and I felt them cool from his touch. "I can teach you to control your reactions. If you would like?"

I nodded. "Please."

"One more thing to add to our list of lessons," he chuckled.

"You spend so much time on me," I whispered, "Why?"

He stepped back, linked his hand with mine, and led me towards the tree. He swept some of the branches aside and held them back so I could walk to the tree's base. With a slow twirl, I spun in a pink cave of flowers. The scent was fresh and my smile spread wider and wider. When I stopped spinning, I found Zydon watching me silently with a smile on his face.

"I've been alive a very long time," he told me. "In that time I have met a lot of people, but for the last two hundred years, we have been living in a bubble and there has been little change. You stumbled into my life and I find everything you do a fresh experience. Simple things like a flower from a field give you joy yet you came from a place that has things beyond my imagination. There is such promise in you and I know that if you had a chance to truly thrive, you would become something great."

So, he spent time with me because I was a shiny new toy.

"You're scowling," he informed me.

"What happens when my 'freshness' has worn off?" I asked skeptically.

He laughed and shook his head. "The silly things you say. Things you are worried about amuse me as well. Your lifetime is a blip compared to mine." He stalked towards me and I could imagine smoke curling from his nostrils and a tail flicking behind him. He was a dragon to me and I could not explain why, aside from his horns. I had backed up so that my back pressed against the trunk of the cherry tree and he leaned towards me with a smile on his face. "I will be wishing and yearning for your presence centuries after you perish," he said, "I would wish every day for one more year, one more day, to spend with you. You've infected me and there is only one cure."

"What's that?" I asked hoarsely, my heart hammering against my chest as the dragon pinned me in the corner.

"To stay by your side for the rest of your life," he answered, placed his hands on either side of me on the tree trunk, and kissed me softly.

The ferocity in his statement and his presence was so at odds with the tenderness of his kiss that I froze momentarily. After recovering, I let my hands slide up his forearms, up his biceps and shoulders, and around his neck. His lips seared mine and I realized that he wasn't the only one affected, possibly permanently.

He broke away sometime later and smiled happily at me. "I worried that you would not return my affection."

"The King of Enki'l was worried about being turned down by a therian?" I teased.

Instead of replying, he kissed me again.

"Did you take me away from the castle so that the others wouldn't know if you were turned down?" I asked as I snaked out from under him.

"No," he replied.

The blossoms were soft as I ran my fingertips over them. If I brought a piece of branch back to the castle, could I get it to grow?

"You have no idea the affect you have on us," he told me as he followed my movements, walking on the opposite side of the branches so that I only saw him when I moved the branches.

"Us?" I asked.

He nodded. "I've seen the way the others look at you."

"And does it make you jealous?" I asked with a screen of blossoms separating us.

"It did," he admitted, "I thought of you with one of them and it made me very jealous."

"Now?" I asked.

He parted the branches and stroked a finger down my cheek. "Now, it will make me smile to know that they may look at you, but you chose me."

"Perhaps I was too hasty in my selection," I teased him and backed away from the tree.

He growled softly and followed me. "Really? And who would you choose instead?"

"I don't know. Lars is handsome and very nice to me," I said. I turned away from him, clasped my hands behind my back and strolled through the forest, its darkness no longer frightening now that Zydon was at my back.

"I could easily defeat him."

"There's also Jeff," I suggested. "He's very intimidating and might make the others think twice before trying anything with me."

"And I'm someone they would not fear?" he asked me in disbelief.

I shrugged and turned around to face him, still walking backwards. "I don't know. Since I haven't had much interaction with others from this island, I don't know if you are feared or not. For all I know, Jeff is the most feared Enki'l in existence."

"Ask the next being you meet what I'm called," he ordered me. "Then you'll see the fallacy in your words."

I laughed loudly and clutched at my stomach as I continued, unable to stop.

He grabbed me around the waist and I swallowed my laughter as I tilted my chin up to look at him. "You are an interesting creature, Celwyn."

"As are you, Zydon."

His lips twisted up and then he pressed them to mine. "We should head back. It is going to be dark soon."

How long had we been here? I looked up, but the canopy of the forest blocked out the sunlight completely, if there was any. My stomach was rumbling, but that wasn't any real indication of how long we had been out.

"Could I contact Chuck somehow from out here?" I requested.

"Are you sure?" he asked me.

"Is it safe? If it's not safe we won't do it, but if..."

He held up his hand. "It's safe. I just don't want you to do something you do not wish to."

"I should at least let him know that I am safe and to let my parents know so that they can relax. My mom is probably worried sick."

He walked to the horses, took out a mirror with a gold handle, and whispered to it softly. It began to glow and he handed it to me quickly before he jogged some ways away from me. I opened my mouth to ask what he was doing, but he just pointed at the mirror.

The mirror's surface swirled a moment and then Chuck's face came into view.

"Chuck," I whispered in shock.

His eyes widened and he asked, "Celwyn?"

I nodded. "I need to talk to you."

"Where are you? I'll send a group out to bring you back."

"I'm not coming back," I told him in my best adult voice.

"What are you talking about? You have to come back. This is your home."

"They tried to kill me," I snapped. "They almost succeeded. That is not my home."

"Who was it?" he asked with a growl. "Whoever it was, I will punish them and..."

"I'm not going to tell you, but I can't go back to the Hall of

Jackals because I know they will seek out other times and I won't live out the year. They made sure to let me know that they were not the only ones who felt this way."

"I can protect…"

"No! I'm not coming back and that's final. Disown me or kick me out, whatever you need to do. Tell Dad and Mom that I'm okay and not to come look for me," I told him.

"Too late," Mauricio said from beside me.

I gasped in shock and almost dropped the mirror. "What are you doing here?"

"I'm here to bring you back," he said.

I backed away from him and shook my head. "I don't want to go back."

"It's not your choice," Mauricio told me. "Either you come back with me, or I kill you."

"Chuck," I gasped.

"Come back," Chuck ordered me. "Let me help you."

"I don't want your help. I want to be left alone and allowed to live!" I yelled at him.

"Last chance," Mauricio said, "Come with me or I kill you for being a traitor."

I shook my head and backed away.

"I didn't want to do this," he said with a sigh. "I'll make your death swift and as painless as possible."

"You won't do anything to her," Zydon said angrily.

"Enki'l!" Mauricio gasped.

"Leave the girl alone," Zydon ordered him.

"Do you realize what she is?" Mauricio asked him. "She's a Therian!"

"Leave these woods and don't come back," Zydon snarled, "This is my territory and you are threatening a member of my house."

"She's a member of the Pack and it's my duty to deal with her. I cannot leave without taking care of her first."

"She stopped being a member of the Pack when they tried to kill her!" Zydon snapped.

"She must die!" Mauricio yelled.

"Last warning," Zydon said.

"Now!" Mauricio bellowed.

Three wolves ran into the clearing and surrounded me. They were different colors, but all massive and snarling at me. I couldn't tell who they were, but it didn't really matter. I was terrified. I had nowhere to go.

"Celwyn!" Zydon yelled.

"She's ours to deal with as we like," Mauricio told him. He faced the wolves and said, "Finish her."

What could defeat three wolves? What animal? What would be the hardest for them to hurt? I closed my eyes and shifted into a hawk and flew up into the sky.

"No!" Mauricio yelled.

The wolves leapt up, trying to bite me, but I was too high up already. I screeched as I flew away from them, looking down to make sure Zydon was fleeing as well. He was on his horse with mine following right behind. When we were a distance from Mauricio and it looked like we had lost them, I stopped and shifted into a tiger, just in case they were still following. Zydon rode past me, guiding me out of the forest and towards the castle. I shifted into a bird, flew to Zydon, and shifted into a fox before curling myself up in his lap on his saddle.

"See, you aren't helpless," he whispered to me.

I squawked at him.

"Your black ears remind me of our horns," he commented with a smile and stroked the tip of one of my ears.

He urged the horses on and soon we were in the field of grass again and the castle was in sight.

"I let Mauricio go," Zydon told me. "We may get a visit or they may leave it alone. The Pack won't want to get into a war with us, especially when their numbers are just as low as ours."

I couldn't respond since I was in fox form, so I just squawked again and watched as the castle grew nearer. Could this be my home? Could I stay here forever? Would Zydon let me stay here?

One day at a time. I had to just deal with it one day at a time. Would Chuck leave me alone now? Or would he continue to talk to me? I hoped he would leave me alone now, but I had no way of knowing what he would do. I did not truly know him and I had no idea what his motives were. Was it possible for him to hurt me through the connection? Or could the Alpha? I had not even thought about that until now. The castle came into view and I sat up straight to get a better look at it. The castle was massive, but surrounding it was a giant moat, making the castle look more like an island than a castle with a moat. The strange thing was that the moat was a perfect circle. It was obviously man made, or Enki'l made more likely. We rode over the bridge and then it was immediately drawn up.

Lars was in the courtyard waiting for us and when he saw me with Zydon, he exhaled loudly. "Things went well?" he asked.

Zydon stopped his horse and I hopped down, still in my fox form. "Not exactly," Zydon said.

I trotted up the steps towards the door and then waited for them to join me. This form was fun to be in. Perhaps I needed to start shifting more to get used to various forms. They could be very useful in a fight. If I'd been a tiger or something I might have been able to defeat the wolves. There might have been some form that was even more powerful.

Jeff walked out of the armory and looked at me in shock. "When did we get a fox?"

I shifted into my normal form and smirked. "It's just me."

"Why were you in a different form?" he asked and then looked over at Zydon who was catching Lars up on what had happened. Jeff went to join them and instead of waiting for Zydon, I went inside to the dining room.

Lars, Zydon, and Jeff joined me shortly thereafter and while they talked, I gorged myself on food. Why was I so hungry?

"How many times did she shift?" Lars asked.

"Four, I believe," Zydon answered.

"That explains why she's eating so much," Jeff responded.

"Why?" I asked.

"The more you shift, the more energy you use. You need to eat and rest to restore that energy," Zydon explained to me.

I reached up towards my ear and then dropped it sadly. My flower was gone. I hadn't thought about it when I shifted. Why couldn't I keep the flower like I regenerated my clothes?

When I was finally full, I excused myself from the three and went to the kitchen. There were three males and two females working in the back and all stopped when they saw me.

"Um, excuse me, I haven't really met you all yet. I'm Celwyn," I greeted them.

"Aye, we know who you are," one of the females said. She was beautiful, had an hourglass shape that I would kill for, and bright red hair.

"I was wondering if there was any work I might be able to do here?" I asked them.

"Work?" the oldest looking male asked.

I nodded. "Since I'm staying here a bit longer than previously planned, I want to earn my keep, like everyone else. I don't feel right not contributing," I explained.

They all looked at each other and then the red-haired female said, "What skills d'you have?"

"Very few," I admitted, "Where I come from, we don't do our chores by hand."

"How do you do them?" the oldest male asked.

"We have machines that do them for us," I explained.

"Magic?" he asked.

I shook my head. "Mechanical or electric. It's hard to explain, but I am willing to learn and I don't mind getting dirty."

They looked at each other again and the oldest male said, "The dishes are always piling up. Come tomorrow morning and I will show you what to do."

I smiled happily and bowed my head. "Thank you."

When I turned around I found Zydon watching me from the doorway. The others hadn't seen him until I turned either and the tension skyrocketed. He didn't say anything though, so I walked past him and out to the hallway towards my room.

After a long bath and some time in front of my fireplace, I went for a walk around the castle. There were so many places that I had walked past, but never explored and I wanted to learn the layout as quickly as possible. Since I wasn't certain which doors were to living quarters, I didn't go inside any door that was not open.

The day with Zydon had been wonderful. It would have been perfect if Mauricio hadn't ruined it. My fingertips stroked the top of my ear where the flower had been and I sighed softly, missing its presence. It would have died after a few days anyway, but that didn't mean that I missed it any less. Being distracted, I had started down a passageway that was barely lit and it became harder for me to see. There were whispering sounds up ahead and I stumbled upon two Enki'l huddled together talking. When they saw me, they stopped talking immediately and hurried around the corner.

What had that been about? Clearly they were talking about me.

"Lost?" Jeff asked loudly in his deep, booming voice.

I yelped in shock and spun around with a hand to my chest. "Don't do that!" I bellowed at him.

He smiled and bowed. "My apologies."

"I was trying to get more familiar with the layout of the castle and I stumbled upon a couple whispering conspiratorially, apparently about me because they disappeared when they saw me."

"Did you recognize them?" Jeff asked.

I shook my head.

"Well, let's get you back to your room. Zydon wouldn't let me hear the end of it if I left you here and you wandered around lost the rest of the evening," he said.

I laughed softly and followed him back down the hallway. One more glance back at the end of the hallway gave me no more clues as to who those two were or what they were talking about. Maybe I was just being paranoid and had disrupted a lover's discussion. Or, was I right to be paranoid?

CHAPTER SIX

D oing dishes by hand wasn't so bad, but doing the massive stacks of dishes that the Enki'l made each day was a huge task I had not been prepared for.

By midday my fingers were prunes and my feet were pounding in pain from standing most of the day. I sat on a staircase and rubbed my feet, muttering to myself about getting dishwashers moved here as soon as possible.

"Good afternoon," Zydon greeted me.

I turned and smiled up at him. "Hello."

He sat beside me and looked at my foot in my hand. "What's wrong?"

"They are just sore because I'm not used to standing all day," I admitted to him. "They'll be sturdier after a week."

He reached out, grabbed my foot, and before I could protest, began rubbing it slowly. I moaned and let my head fall back as his hands expertly kneaded my feet.

"I thought you might be hiding," he told me.

"Why would I be hiding?" I asked.

"Regret," he suggested.

I leaned over and kissed his cheek. "No."

He reached off to the side and then placed a replica of the flower he had given me yesterday on top of my ear.

I smiled happily and said, "Thank you."

"I noticed you reach for it at dinner last night and thought you might like to have another one."

"Very perceptive," I teased him. I leaned over and kissed his lips lightly. "Thank you."

"Will you have time to meet me for dinner tonight?" he asked.

"I suppose I could make time for you," I said as though it were a big chore.

"I could order you to eat dinner with me," he reminded me.

"Ah, but what fun would it be to force a woman to eat with you," I said and stood up. "I think you enjoy the chase."

"Chases do not last long when I'm the hunter," he said with a dragon's smile.

I swallowed and when I finally found my voice said, "I look forward to dinner."

He stood and kissed my cheek. "As do I." He bowed and said, "Until tonight, my lady."

I watched him walk away and wondered if I had gotten in over my head. I smiled and nodded my head. Definitely.

I walked out to the courtyard, humming happily, and stopped in front of Lars who had been waiting for me.

"You're late," he scolded me.

"Sorry," I apologized, but couldn't stop from smiling.

"You seem to be in a good mood."

I nodded. "I've been working in the kitchen all day."

"That makes you happy?" he asked, confused.

"I'm earning my keep," I explained.

"I am fairly certain that our King would allow you to live here for free," he said with a smirk.

"I don't like being a burden, so it makes me feel good to do something here."

"Well, let's get to your training. The quicker you become a soldier, the more ways you can earn your keep."

I was not certain what he meant by that, but I decided not to question him. I had asked plenty of questions these last couple of weeks. He led me through some fighting stances and moves and then handed me my sword.

"Raise the sword up over your head with both hands holding the hilt," he ordered me. I did as he asked and he nodded. "Now, bring it down in front of you hard, like you're trying to strike someone or cut a melon in half, but stop when the sword is at about your belly button."

I brought the sword down and he shook his head. "Faster and harder. Imagine a melon on a table and the only way to cut it is to use this sword. You have to do it in one strike."

I tried again and he smiled. "Yes. Now, every day I want you to do this move fifty times. Got it?"

I nodded and raised the sword again.

"Lars!" Jeff called from near the drawbridge.

Lars raised his hand in acknowledgment. "I'll be back. Keep going until you hit your fifty, okay?"

I nodded and took deep, slow breaths as I did the movements over and over again. My arms grew tired quickly and my hands were sweaty. I had to dry my palms off on my pants a couple times so that I did not drop my sword.

Zydon walked out of the dining hall and headed towards the drawbridge. What was happening?

Instead of making myself a pest like I wanted to, I continued my strikes. To become strong, I had to build up my endurance and strength and to do that I had to practice. Stopping every time that I thought something interesting might be going on would only hinder me. There would be plenty of time for resting and making a pest out of myself later, after I had proven myself.

"Where is she!" a familiar voice bellowed. Chuck. It was Chuck.

I set my sword in the stand in front of the armory and shifted into a hawk. With a few hard flaps, I rose up into the air and to the top of the castle where I could see everything. I landed on the part above the draw bridge and looked down in shock at Chuck, Merle, and Dad standing on the far side of the moat while Lars, Jeff, and Zydon stood on the inside of the drawbridge.

"She's alive and safe," Zydon told them, "Which is more than I can say you provided her."

"She is part of our pack," Merle reminded him.

"She requested separation," Zydon reminded him.

"She can't just leave," Chuck said.

"Is the pack keeping members as prisoners now?" Lars asked angrily.

"Bring me my daughter," Dad ordered them.

"No," Jeff said.

Dad shifted into a half wolf half man form and growled at them. If I didn't stop them, they would fight and someone would get hurt. I could not let them get hurt over me. I screeched and flew down, circling to land in front of Zydon who scowled at me. After shifting, I turned and faced my Dad and the others.

"I'm perfectly safe," I told them. "You have no business being here."

"You belong to the Pack," Merle told me.

"I don't belong to anyone!" I yelled at him. "I joined your Pack, followed all of your rules and was almost killed for it! If Zydon had not found me, I would be dead right now. Then what would you be doing, huh? You wouldn't be doing anything because there is nothing you could have done."

"I tried to protect you," Chuck reminded me.

"I know and I appreciate everything you have done for me, but I can't return. They made it clear that they won't accept a Therianthrope in their midst."

"And you think we can accept you leaving us to help our enemy?" Merle asked me.

"When did we become your enemy?" Zydon asked, "Last I checked, we saved your asses from Adbalh."

"Why do you want her?" Merle asked him. "If not to use her for your own advantage?"

Zydon growled and took a step forward, but I blocked his path. "He's trying to provoke you," I said.

"It's working and he won't like the result," he said. His eyes were glowing and it looked like smoke was rising from his skin.

"Your mother is worried sick," Dad said, "Come home."

"I am home," I said and turned around to face him. "Tell Mom I love her and perhaps in the future I will send communication to her, but I'm not leaving."

"I'm sorry, Tyren," Merle said and sighed. "I didn't want it to come to this." He pulled something out of his pocket that looked like a pen. Dad yelled and leapt towards him at the same time that Zydon yelled my name and reached for me.

My head felt like it exploded and I hit the ground before I could even reach up. Coldness surrounded me and I lay paralyzed.

"Celwyn!" Zydon yelled. He sounded like he was yelling at me through a paper towel roll underwater. He picked me up and moved me, but I felt none of it, only saw the sky move.

Where was Dad? Was he okay? What had happened? Why couldn't I move?

My mouth wouldn't open and I couldn't make sound. Was I dead?

"Celwyn, can you hear me?" Lars asked.

"Why isn't she moving?" Jeff asked.

"Stay with me Celwyn," Zydon ordered me. "Stay with me."

"What did he use? What was that thing?" Lars asked.

"If she dies, I will hunt him down and tear him apart," Zydon snarled.

Then I wasn't dead, yet. How could I let them know I could hear them?

"What can we do?" Jeff asked.

"Get the healers, all of them," Zydon ordered.

Jeff and Lars made sounds of acknowledgement and disappeared. The sky disappeared and the ceiling of the castle appeared above me and then my bedroom ceiling.

Zydon leaned over me and pressed his forehead to mine. "Stay with me, Celwyn. Don't leave me so soon."

"What's happened?" someone asked.

"Her eyes are open and she's breathing, but her heartbeat is slowing," Zydon informed them.

"What was the spell or weapon?" the person asked. It sounded like Sanora, but I was not completely certain.

"Loup Dart," Zydon said softly.

"Then why is she frozen?" Lars asked.

"I don't know. Perhaps it doesn't work on her the same way because she's a Therianthrope and not a Werewolf," Zydon suggested.

"Where's the wound?" one of the healers asked.

"Her sternum," Zydon said.

"Everyone out," the healer ordered, "Let us work."

"I'm not leaving," Zydon informed them.

"As you wish, King," Sanora acknowledged.

There were tearing sounds and movement all around me, but I did not know what was going on. I hated not knowing. Something cool leaked into my veins and my eyes fluttered, trying to close.

"We're losing her!" one of the healers yelled.

"Celwyn!" Zydon yelled. "Fight it, Celwyn. You can fight this. You are stronger than this!"

"Flush the wound out."

"Where's the wolfsbane?"

The healers barked orders and moved around frantically. My lungs squeezed tighter and tighter and soon I was gasping for breath. I did not want to die. I was young. I had so much life left. I had barely seen anything or experienced anything.

Those stupid Shifters would not kill me. I would not let them win! I was strong. I would not let this island defeat me so soon or so easily. I was not a werewolf. This Loup Dart would not kill me.

My eyes closed and though I heard Zydon and the healers, they sounded far away.

"Wake up, child," a woman's voice said, "I have use of you yet and your journey has only just begun."

"Who are you?" I asked. There was no light or movement.

"A friend and a guardian who is vested in your life. Your Enki'l is using long forgotten magic to keep you alive. Wake up, girl. Wake up and become the Queen you should be!"

I bolted upright and inhaled a giant breath of air. My heart raced and my lungs greedily drank down and expelled air.

"What?"

"How?"

"Celwyn."

I opened my eyes and looked at the three healers and Zydon. "I won't die so easily," I whispered and then fell into a deep, peaceful sleep.

Two days later, I awoke with one side of my face sweating and stuck to something warm. I raised my head and stared in surprise at a shirtless and sleeping Zydon. My head had been resting on his chest, where a slimy spot still lay. I grimaced and used the bottom of my shirt to wipe the sweat, and hopefully not drool, off.

Zydon stirred and then opened his eyes. "Celwyn," he whispered in shock and sat up. "How do you feel?"

"Thirsty," I croaked.

He rested his forehead against mine a moment and then went to the side table where a pitcher and glass sat.

"I thought you might never wake up," he told me softly as he handed me the glass of water.

Slowly, I drank the water and once I had fully satiated my thirst, I said, "I'm sorry to have worried you."

"It was my fault," he said. He hugged me, pet my hair, and whispered, "I failed to protect you like I promised."

"It was not your fault," I assured him. "It was Merle's."

He growled, the rumble vibrated my ear where it lay against his chest. "If he ever crosses my lands again, I'm going to kill him."

"My Dad is he..."

"He's fine. They left after we took you inside. I let your father know that you had survived but were still unconscious."

"How did I survive?" I asked. The woman in my dream had said something about him using a magic.

"It's been a long time since I've had to use magic on humans," he said, "But I remember some of the old magic."

"What did you do?" I asked.

"I helped you fight the Loup Dart," he said. "You were the one who actually did it."

I shook my head. "A woman spoke to me," I told him, "She said you were using a long-lost magic to keep me alive."

"It was nothing," he said, but somehow, I knew he was lying.

"I'm sorry I caused you trouble again," I apologized.

"Shut up," he ordered me. "No more apologizing."

"Yes, my King," I whispered.

He pushed me back and frowned at me. "What?"

"Um, aren't you?" I inquired.

He shook his head. "No, to you I am just Zydon."

"Oh," I whispered sadly. I thought he would accept me here. Clearly, I misunderstood his feelings. Hadn't he said I was part of his house?

"Let's get you changed and then get you some food. You're probably hungry," he said.

"Right," I agreed.

"And I can let the others know you're fine so they can stop pacing trenches in my hallways," he said with a soft laugh. "Everyone has been worried about you."

I nodded and let him help me stand and walk to the bathroom. He set a change of clothes on the counter for me and then shut the door to give me privacy. Was I wrong? I thought he wanted me here? Why wouldn't he be my King then?

"Everything alright?" Zydon called.

"Yeah," I answered and glared at my reflection. Later, I would think about this all later after I put a smile on my face and let everyone know that I was alive and well.

When we stepped outside of my room, Lars and Jeff rushed towards us.

"Celwyn!"

"Celwyn!"

I stepped away from Zydon and hugged them both. "I'm okay, I promise. I guess I just needed a long nap."

"I'm glad you're doing well," Lars said and patted the top of my head. "It's been too quiet with you sleeping."

"Better than me waking you up wailing," I reminded him.

His smile slipped and he said, "I would have preferred that to you being unconscious so long."

I bumped him with my shoulder and said, "Come on, gloomy puss, let's get some grub. I'm famished."

"Are you sure you can walk?" Zydon asked me.

I shrugged. "We'll find out." With Lars on my left, Zydon on my right, and Jeff behind me, we walked down the hallway slowly, but I made it to the dining hall on my own and without a single fall. A major victory in my mind.

"Celwyn!" several voices called out as we entered.

"We've been so worried," a few said as we took seats at one of the table. There were around twenty males and two females in the room, none of them had food in front of them which meant we made it in time for the food. I had met several of them many times, but I was terrible with names and could not remember any of theirs. On top of earning my keep and becoming stronger, I needed to get to know the Enki'l better.

"Thank you," I said and fought to keep from tearing up at their honest worry over me, "I'm feeling much better now."

Food was served and I ate and ate and ate, never filling full or satisfied.

"Easy," Zydon warned me, "You don't want to make yourself throw up and then waste all that food that you ate."

"I'm just so hungry," I told him. "I feel like I haven't even started eating yet."

"Drink some water," Lars suggested. "You need to get rehydrated."

"Did anything happen while I was asleep?" I inquired.

Lars looked at Zydon who shook his head. "Nothing of consequence."

"So, something did happen then," I said and focused on Lars who was still looking at Zydon.

"How are you feeling?" Zydon asked.

"I feel hungry and tired. Why am I still tired?" It worried me, especially since I had slept for so long.

"Your body uses up a lot of energy when it is healing itself," Lars said.

"Yeah, but didn't Zydon use his magic to heal me?" I reminded him. Surely if Zydon had used his magic to heal me, I wouldn't have used as much of my energy as normally expected for recovery.

"His magic?" Lars questioned. "What are you talking about?" Lars looked at Zydon. "What is she talking about?"

"She had a dream and thinks that I used some type of magic to heal her," he explained, "But it was only the healers who used magic on her."

He was lying. I knew somehow that he was lying. Even if that had just been a dream, he did use his magic to heal me.

"I feel like all I've done since coming here is lie around and try to recover," I complained. "I'm going to go for a walk."

"You don't want to push yourself," Zydon warned me.

"Yes," I replied and stood up. "I do." I walked out of the dining hall well aware that I was the center of attention and every single being was staring after me. A walk would help me clear my head and try to figure out and process everything. I walked halfway around the castle and then paused in one of the side hallways.

"If you keep frowning like that, you'll develop wrinkles," the red-haired female Enki'l who worked in the kitchen with me said. Her name was Sherce and she was incredibly fast with the dishes.

"Hi, Sherce," I greeted her.

"I'm glad that you are doing well," she said.

"Yeah, it's been a rough month," I said and laughed bitterly.

"Will you be in the kitchen tomorrow?"

I nodded. "Definitely."

"What's troubling you?" she asked me.

"This world is so different from mine," I told her, "And I don't know what to think or do. It's overwhelming."

"I can understand that," she said and sat down on stairs to our left. I sat beside her with a sigh. "You have definitely made an impact on the lives of the Enki'l."

"I've caused you all a lot of trouble. Hopefully there won't be anything else in the future."

"We can hope," she agreed. "Perhaps you will find your soul mate."

"I don't believe in soul mates," I told her.

"You don't?" she asked, shocked.

I shook my head. "No."

"When a soul is created, it is split in two and placed into two beings. Then they search across the world and time so that they can find each other. When they are reunited and acknowledge their connection, special power is unlocked in them both," she explained.

"That is an interesting story," I told her.

"It's not just a story, it is reality."

"Have you seen soulmates reunited?" I asked.

She nodded. "Yes. It's a beautiful thing to witness."

"So you believe every person has a soulmate?"

She shook her head. "No, not everyone. That is why it is so special."

"So, it is possible that I do not have a soulmate?"

She smiled. "I have a feeling about you. I firmly believe you have a soulmate."

I had no idea what to say regarding that statement and I just laughed.

She stood up and dusted off the back of her pants. "Laugh all you want, but when you finally accept your soulmate, you better come back and give me a present."

Her discussion had distracted me and calmed me down. No one was in the courtyard and instead of sitting in the courtyard, I shifted into a hawk and flew up into the night's sky. Circling a few times above the courtyard, I caught sight of Lars who saw me as well. Before he could tell me to come down, I flew out over the walls, past the moat, and skimmed low over the grasses.

Animals moved around the grasses and in the forest beyond, hunting and going about their nocturnal lives. Their lives were so simple and yet just as dangerous as mine, maybe more. The wind blew underneath my wings, pushing me along. I dipped and then swooped up again, climbing higher and higher. I flew around for an hour and then shifted into my normal form and walked towards the castle, running my fingers through the grass.

"A Shifter," a nasally voice said, "So far from home. What are you doing here, little Shifter?"

I turned around, but could not find the speaker. "Who's there? What do you want?"

"Do you know where you are? This is the Devil of Olansia's territory."

"I'm here on his invitation," I said. "I was just taking a short stroll."

"It's unfortunate for you," he said, "Since you are out here and he won't know that you're dead until the morning."

I backed up towards the castle and scanned the area around me. Where was he? I shifted into a bird and began to fly up, but something grabbed my leg and pulled me down.

"Where do you think you're going?" he asked.

His face was catlike and he had pointed ears. He was terrifying.

I shifted back and said, "Please! Let me go!"

"The past two hundred years I have been limited in my hunting since my prey has been limited in number. Now that we have returned to this dimension, the prey has returned as well. It's a glorious day for me. Today I will kill you and renew my hunting." He wrapped his hand around my throat and tightened his grip.

I struggled against him and tried to break his grip, but he held firm. He was too strong for me. I should have stayed inside the castle. I wasn't ready to come outside, away from protection yet.

Tendrils of black smoke wrapped around me and then I was able to breathe. I gasped for breath and was shocked that I could breathe in the darkness. Wait? Was I dead? Was the darkness my death?

"Zydon!" my attacker yelled in shock.

"Adbalh Foxkiller, what are you doing on my lands?" Zydon asked in a snarl. The black smoke disappeared and I found myself in Zydon's arms.

"Zydon," I gasped in a hoarse voice.

"Are you alright?" Zydon asked me. He pressed his fingertips to my forehead and his scent surrounded me at the same time that my throat warmed and healed.

"Why do you have a Shifter staying with you?" Adbalh asked.

"It's none of your business. This girl is under my protection. She is a member of my house. Do you understand?"

"She is not supposed to be alive," Adbalh snapped.

"Are you challenging me?" Zydon asked. The black smoke began to rise from his body again, swirling around him and me.

Adbalh snarled, but backed away. "This is not over, girl."

"You will have to go through me to get to her. You have no hopes of defeating me," Zydon said.

Adbalh disappeared into the night, leaving me alone with Zydon.

"I'm sorry. I was just flying and stopped in the grass. I didn't know anyone was out here," I explained quickly.

"It's alright," he said and leaned his forehead against mine. "You should not have been in danger anywhere on my lands. I'm going to have to increase patrols or possibly erect boundaries."

"Is the smoke your power?" I asked.

He nodded and then smiled at me. "Want to see something?" I nodded and the smoke swirled around us until we were completely enveloped, the next moment it was gone and we were in the castle in the courtyard.

"Wow," I gasped.

He set me down and Lars was instantly in front of me, searching me over. "Are you hurt?"

"I'm fine," I assured him.

Lars exhaled and then turned serious. "Don't go out without one of us again!"

I felt like a child being scolded and turned away. "I'm sorry."

"That's enough," Zydon ordered.

"I'm going to go to bed," I told them. "Sorry for causing trouble again." I ran away from the two males and to my room where I collapsed onto my bed and cried.

Three times. Three times I was almost killed. Tomorrow I would work extra hard to become stronger. I had to. I had to become strong enough to walk outside of the castle walls. I could not be a burden to Zydon and the others forever. I had overstayed my welcome as it was. Even if they did not feel that way I felt that way and I needed to do something about it.

"Celwyn?" Zydon whispered, "What's wrong?"

I turned my head to find him kneeling beside the bed with creased eyebrows. I wiped at my eyes and nodded. "I'm fine."

"You're lying," he said. Before I could argue, he lifted me up, sat on the bed, and cradled me in his lap.

"I'm not a child," I snapped and tried to get away.

"Everyone gets scared sometimes," he whispered and stroked my hair, "Adbalh is a frightening male, even for other males."

My lip began to quiver and I shuddered in his hold. "Why did he want to kill me?" I asked and sobbed loudly. "He didn't even know me or who I was."

"Adbalh has only ever had one goal, to exterminate Shifters," he explained. "It's perfectly normal for you to have been scared."

I nodded. He tightened his arms around me and continued petting my hair. "I couldn't do anything. His grip was so tight and no matter how hard I struggled, I couldn't break free," I cried and sobbed against him.

"It's alright, Celwyn. You are safe now. I've got you and I'll always protect you."

My tears continued to flow despite his reassuring words. He

held me until my tears were spent and then curled around me in the bed.

"I thought I was going to die," I whispered as he held me, my tears now subsided. "I didn't think there was any way that you would know I was in trouble. He said that you would not find my body until the next morning and I knew he was most likely right. I would die alone in that field and you would find my cold body the next morning or possibly not for even longer. I didn't want to die alone. I don't want to die alone."

"You're not going to die," he assured me. "You would not have died in the grass. I may not have felt him in my territory, but I knew where you were. I would have been there sooner, but I did not feel that you were in trouble or sense him. I knew as soon as you were in trouble and came as fast as I could."

"How did you know where I was?" I inquired.

He was quiet so long that I thought he was not going to respond. "I told you before that I felt a connection with you. It feels even stronger now."

"What type of connection?" I asked. "What do you mean? Why can't I sense you?"

"You can't sense me?" he asked. "You can't tell when I enter a room?"

"I can sense your aura," I explained.

"You can sense me," he corrected.

"Oh."

"Close your eyes," he instructed. I obeyed. "Do you feel me?" I nodded. "I will always know when you are in trouble, no matter how far away. Now, go to sleep. I will stay here until you are asleep, okay?"

"Thank you."

CHAPTER SEVEN

I spent two weeks training, cleaning dishes, and then eating dinner with the Enki'l soldiers. I was by no means a soldier, but I was improving. Lars trained me for two hours a day and then Zydon trained me for an additional hour on various things. I spent an hour before I fell asleep shifting into various forms and moving around. Sometimes I went out into the courtyard and practiced fighting the straw dummy for practice. Zydon watched me from his balcony occasionally, but never came down to coach me or said anything about my training sessions.

I was halfway into the week and staring at my reflection incredulously. Despite all of my training, I had not gained much muscle. I had lost some excess fat, not that I had much to begin with, but I wanted to fill out more. Zydon had not made any further advances on me, which was incredibly depressing. Was it because I was a Shifter? Did he want an Enki'l?

Closing my eyes, I pictured horns like Zydon had. My magic swirled around me and when I opened my eyes, I had horns on my head and almost looked like an Enki'l.

"What are you doing?" Zydon demanded.

I turned around and gasped. "I didn't know you were there. I didn't hear the door," I stammered. As fast as I could, I made the horns go away and fidgeted with my shirt.

"How many times have you done that?" he inquired.

"Only this once," I answered truthfully. "I just wanted to see what I would look like."

"Don't do that again, please," he requested.

"Why not?"

He smoothed down the hair on the top of my head and said, "Because you're beautiful without horns."

"Am I more beautiful with them?" I asked. "Would you rather I had them?"

"No," he answered instantly. "I prefer you without horns."

"I upset you," I realized. "I'm sorry. I did not mean to offend you." Of course, I had offended him, I had made horns like it was a Halloween costume.

"Promise not to do it again?" he asked.

I nodded and looked up at him. "Did you need something?"

He smiled, nodded, and then kissed me lightly on the lips. "You've been so busy training lately that I haven't been able to spend much time with you."

"You've been training with me," I reminded him.

"Yes, but those are training sessions, not time for me to flirt with you," he explained.

"How chivalrous of you," I teased.

His eyes sparkled and his black smoke swirled around us. "I want to show you something."

The smoke disappeared and we stood on the top of the highest tower of his castle. The moon hung low along the horizon and seemed much larger than usual. Was it the harvest moon? How much time had passed since we left our home?

"It's beautiful," I whispered as we looked out over the horizon.

I could see shapes moving in the grasses and the forest beyond. My heart beat a bit faster as I worried that Adbalh might be out there. Had he left or was he waiting for me to make a mistake again to kill me?

Zydon wrapped his arm around my waist, keeping me from falling. "I don't take time to enjoy it as much as I used to," he admitted. "I thought you would find it beautiful."

I nodded and then looked up at him. "Thank you, for bringing me up here."

"Training diligently is a good thing," he whispered, "but you have to take time away every now and then to decompress."

"Okay."

"Perhaps we can make this a reoccurring event?" he suggested. "Each week I can bring you up here and we can stay here as long as you want."

I leaned into him and said, "I like the sound of that."

We watched the moon rise and then he transported us back to my room. "I've got some things to take care of before I can rest for the night. I'll see you in the morning for breakfast?

I nodded and kissed his cheek. "Good night."

He smiled and left.

"I'm in way over my head," I muttered and then collapsed backwards onto my bed.

Two knocks on my door woke me and I leapt up in shock, not realizing that I had fallen asleep.

"Coming!" I called and hurried to the door. I poked my head out so they could not see my clothes and smiled. "Hello."

Lars stood, frowning at me. "Were you still asleep?"

"Um, yeah. Did I miss our training?"

"It's past midday," he informed me.

I gasped in shock and said, "Give me five minutes to change."

"Zydon was worried about you missing both breakfast and lunch so he asked me to check on you."

"Why didn't he check on me if he was worried?" I grumbled.

"He had some matters to attend to or he would have," he assured me.

"I'll be right out," I said and shut the door. Why had I slept so long? I hadn't felt terribly tired last night? As quickly as I could, I changed clothes, brushed my hair, and brushed my teeth. My hair was frizzy, but I could not do much about it. I decided to braid it quickly to keep it away from my face and out of my eyes.

"Sorry to keep you waiting," I apologized as I stepped out.

"Let's take you to get some food," he said, "And then we will start training."

"What will I be working on today?" I asked. A few Enki'l in the hallways waved to us and a few glared at me. They were probably upset that an outsider was so close to their leader, something I understood.

"More sword training," he confirmed. Once we had past the few people in the hall, he turned to me and asked, "Why are you frowning?"

"It's nothing," I lied.

"Is it because of how they look at you?" he guessed.

"I'm an outsider to them. I have yet to earn any respect here," I said with a shrug.

"What are you planning?" he asked with a snarl afterwards.

I jerked in shock, how had he guessed that I was planning something? Was he that intuitive? Or was I just that obvious?

"I don't know what you're talking about? I'm only planning to work hard on getting stronger." That last part was at least true.

"Whatever it is that you are planning, if it's dangerous, please talk to one of us first. I'd rather not see you almost die again."

I stumbled a step and then stopped.

"I didn't mean to upset you," he said immediately. "I just…"

I shook my head and resumed walking. "Let's just move forward."

"You're sad now," he commented.

"I'll get over it."

"I haven't spent much time with females the past two hundred years," he explained, "So, I forget how my words can affect you.

I'm sorry. I simply meant to say that I would be distraught to have to watch you in pain or to be very ill. I was attempting to make a point that you should not needlessly put yourself in danger."

"I understand," I said. "Don't worry about it."

"What did you do to make her upset?" Jeff asked.

Lars sighed. "How long have you been following us?"

"Not long," Jeff admitted.

"Why were you following us?" I asked without turning to look at him.

"Zydon sent me to check on you to report back to him," he explained.

"I'm well," I answered. "I don't know why I slept so much, but that's all that happened. I overslept."

"She was asleep until I went and woke her up by knocking," Lars informed him.

"Sleeping for that long?" Jeff asked. "That's not a good sign."

"I feel fine," I assured them. "I'm just hungry and feel bad for missing my trainings this morning."

"I'll be back," Jeff said and then disappeared in black smoke like Zydon.

"Is that an Enki'l power?" I asked Lars.

"Only the most powerful of us can use it," he explained. "Zydon is the most powerful. We can only use it for short transportation whereas he can take multiple people across far distances with it."

"Amazing," I whispered. "What else does the black smoke let you do?"

Lars smirked. "I'm not sure I can give those secrets away just yet."

"Why not? I'm not going to tell anyone?" I asked sadly. Even Lars didn't trust me.

"I think our King enjoys surprising you with new tricks," Lars said.

We stepped into the dining room and took seats at the table. "You don't have to sit with me while I eat," I told Lars. "I can just meet you after I'm done eating."

"I'm worried about how much you slept. I want to keep an eye on you to be sure that you really are alright and just needed some extra sleep," he explained.

"I'm not a child," I mumbled.

Greydon, the head chef, brought out two plates of food for me. "You finally woke up, eh?" he asked.

"Sorry," I whispered, "I guess I just needed some extra sleep."

"It happens to us all occasionally," he said with a shrug. "I brought you some extra food and those packed with protein."

"Thank you."

"You said it happens to you all occasionally," Lars said. "What did you mean by that?"

"The staff and I have days where that happens. It's rare, maybe once a year, but we've all experienced it," he explained.

"Is it just the serving staff?" Lars asked.

Greydon frowned and looked at the floor. "I don't know. I'm pretty sure, but I hadn't really thought about it. I just assumed everyone experienced it."

"What happens the next day after you sleep?" Lars asked.

Greydon smiled and said, "You eat a lot and then return to normal."

"I'll be right back, stay here until I get back," Lars said and then disappeared in a swirl of smoke.

"He looked worried," I whispered.

"That he did," Greydon agreed. "I wouldn't think about it too much, Celwyn. Eat your food and let me know if you need more."

"Thank you!" I called as he walked away and then dug into my food. It was wonderful tasting and I ate every last piece. I could have asked for more, but decided not to bother Greydon.

I felt him the instant he entered the room. I didn't move or let him know that I had noticed though.

"Red is a good color on you," Zydon whispered from beside me.

"Thank you," I replied and turned around with a smile on my face.

"You felt me, didn't you?" he asked.

"Maybe," I admitted.

"So, your connection is working," he whispered and sounded relieved.

"I only felt you when you entered the room," I told him. "I could not feel you when you were wherever you were in the castle."

"It's an improvement," he said happily.

"To what do I owe the pleasure of your company?" I asked him.

"I need to scan you," he informed me.

"Scan me?" I asked. What did that mean? Like a CT-scan?

"Don't worry, it won't hurt," he assured me. He pushed my chair back so that I was fully facing him and then moved forward so his knees were on the outside of mine. He leaned forward and kissed my lips lightly, running his fingertips down the side of my body, from the top of my head, to my hip. My body tingled all over and I shivered from the feeling.

"What was that?" I asked breathlessly.

"Me scanning your body," he explained.

"For what?"

"To see if there were any noticeable illnesses, or magic spells placed on you," he said nonchalantly.

"Were there?" I asked nervously.

He smiled and rested his hand on my cheek. "I would not be this calm if there had been."

I exhaled and let my head drop forward. "That's a relief."

"Though, I did pick up on something," he said.

I jerked my head up and asked, "What?"

He shrugged. "I'm not sure what it is. It doesn't appear to be negatively affecting you and I can't touch it."

"Does it have to do with the Shifters?" They had not been in contact with us since, but that did not mean that they had given up on trying to kill me.

"No," he assured me, "Though you are still connected to them."

"Can't you remove it?" I begged. "Please?"

He shook his head. "No, I'm sorry. I can't."

"You can," I reminded him and stood up. "You just won't."

He grabbed my hand and stopped me. "Celwyn..."

"It's not your job to remove it," I said and smiled at him. "I don't expect you to. I'll just have to find another way to remove my connection."

"There is not a safe way to remove it without some permanent change," he explained.

"Perhaps a permanent change is what I need," I suggested and then shrugged. "We'll see what options present themselves. I'm late to my training."

He let me leave and I promised myself that I would do all that I could to break this connection. I did not want to be connected to the Shifters any longer. How could I break free?

Lars was not at the courtyard, so I picked up my sword and began my strength training and practice moves. When I had finished and he still hadn't returned, I decided to go back to my room to bathe. The warm water felt incredible on my sore muscles and I drifted between consciousness and unconsciousness as I soaked in it.

"You have to find the necklace," a woman's voice whispered.

"What?" I gasped and sat up. There was no one in the room as I looked around, but I had definitely heard something.

Was I going crazy? That would be a perfect addition to this stupid year. Oh, you're not only a shapeshifter, but you're also weak, worthless, and crazy. Wonderful. This was definitely something I was not going to tell Zydon.

The voice did not come again. I had obviously imagined it. The stress of everything was definitely getting to me. Soon I would get into a rhythm of life here and then...life here? Would I stay here?

Shaking my head, I scolded myself. One day at a time. One. Day. At. A. Time.

My sleep was fitful as images of a castle ruin with a woman trapped under the rubble. She called out to me for help, but I could not get close enough to the ruin to get her out.

"Your mind is elsewhere," Lars accused. "What are you thinking of during the middle of practice?"

"I'm sorry," I apologized and gripped my dagger tighter.

"That's enough for today," he said and put his dagger away. "You'll only get injured if you're distracted."

Arguing would do no good against Lars, he was more stubborn than Zydon.

"Do you want to talk about it?" Lars asked.

"I just had a strange dream last night," I explained, "And I can't stop thinking about it."

"What was it about?"

"Uh, castle ruins somewhere," I tried to explain. "There was a woman trapped and I could not get her out. She kept calling me, but I could never get closer to the ruins to help her."

"Ruins?" Jeff asked. He looked at Lars. "Could she be talking about the ruins of Liana?"

"Who is Liana?" I asked and tried to pretend that Jeff had not startled me by his sudden intrusion into our conversation. I really was distracted.

"She was a Shifter. She should have been the leader of the Shifters actually, but she never took that role. She was one of the five Celestial Tigers," Jeff explained.

"Tigers? I didn't know there were tiger Shifters."

Lars laughed and shook his head. "No, she wasn't a tiger Shifter, she was one of the five most powerful beings in all the lands."

"Wow. What happened to her?" Obviously, she wasn't alive any longer.

"I don't know," Lars admitted. "Zydon might know."

"Know what?" Zydon asked as he walked towards us, across the courtyard.

He had on a tight black shirt and you could see every ripple of his muscles through it. Bless whoever made it and gave it to him.

"Did you know Liana?" I asked as I fought not to drool. Drooling was not ladylike. Okay, I wasn't ladylike to begin with, but it was still frowned upon to drool in front of men.

He nodded. "I did."

"What happened to her?"

He looked up at the cloudless sky and said, "We felt the world changing. We weren't certain what was going to happen, but we all knew it was going to be terrible. For weeks, we all gathered and tried to figure out what to do, but without knowing what was going to happen, it was like finding a needle in a haystack.

"Right before the magic disappeared, we gathered and all used our power to send Olansia to another dimension. It took a lot out of the five of us. I was out for a week. *Name looked like she would pull through, but ultimately she could not recoup her strength and she died."

"How sad," I whispered. "To go through all of that, to save your people and then die."

"She died for her people," he said. "Her sacrifice was not in vain."

"What kind of Shifter was she?" Not that it mattered to me, but I was curious.

"Lion," he responded and then frowned at all of us. "Why are you asking me about Liana? What brought this up?"

Lars and Jeff looked at me expectantly. Barely able to keep

from fidgeting, I smiled and said, "No reason," and then walked away as fast as I could. They could tell him about my dream if they wanted, but I needed to go wash off the sweat that was sticking to me.

After my bath, I lay on my bed in a robe, and stared up at the ceiling. Something was telling me that I had to go find these ruins. Liana had something to do with me. I wasn't certain if it was a good thing or not, but I had to find out.

At dinner, I noticed Zydon looking at me. He tilted his head to the side, gesturing me to follow him out. I excused myself from the conversation that had been going on with Lars, Jeff, and a couple others. After snagging one more roll it took a bit of maneuvering to dodge and weave around the few drunken Enki'l.

Zydon stood across the hallway, upper back leaned against the wall, his left leg bent so that his foot pushed against the wall as well. The shirt he was wearing clung to his biceps and stomach, accentuated his wide back, and would make even men stop to appreciate his physique.

"You summoned me, My King?" I asked and curtsied.

"I can't go with you to the ruins, if that is where you are planning to go," he informed me.

"Why not?" I asked nervously. Traveling without him was terrifying to think about. What if the Shifters found me? What if Adbalh found me?

"I have sworn never to return to those ruins. If you go, you will have to go without me."

"Okay," I replied sadly. I had to go, no matter what. Even if it meant putting my life on the line.

"You are still going to go?" he questioned in disbelief.

"Yes. I can't explain it, but I just know that I have to go to the ruins. There is something there for me or for me to find."

"Your dream could have just been a dream," he snapped.

"I don't know what to say," I admitted.

"Say that you won't go. Say that you will stay here," he urged me.

"Will…will I be allowed to return?" That possibility had not even occurred ot me until talking to him just now. Should I go if he said I could not come back?

"You will always have a place here," he assured me.

I exhaled in relief and looked down at the floor.

He hugged me firmly and whispered, "Please, reconsider. You don't know the way and you aren't ready to face the dangers of Olansia."

"I doubt that I will ever be ready to face everything that Olansia has," I agreed.

"I have to take care of something tonight. Will you meet me for breakfast tomorrow?" he requested.

I looked up at him and smiled. "Breakfast with the King is always something I look forward to."

He laughed softly and kissed my lips. "Sweet dreams, beautiful."

Practically skipping down the hallway, I made it to my room and began to pack the necessities I would need for my trip. The first thing I would need to get from someone was a map. Maybe Zydon would let me borrow a horse? Food! What was I going to do about food?

I was so unprepared. Was I being stupid by going? What if it was a trap? No, I was certain that it was not a trap. I did not believe in destiny, but I had to do this.

It took a bit of searching and begging to find some clothes fitting for a long trip through unknown territory. Greydon provided me with a small sack of dried meats and bread for my trip as well as a canteen for water.

It had taken me a long time getting dressed that morning and I had opted for my jeans, a pair of knee high boots, and a tank top I had cut out of a large shirt I had found. Zydon sat on the far side of the table in the dining room, a sour expression on his face as he glared down at the table top.

"What has happened so early this morning to give you that sour expression?" I asked him and took my seat.

He looked up at smiled at me. "Worrying over things that have yet to pass," he admitted. He looked at my outfit and asked, "You are still going?"

"Zydon, I told you that I was going."

"I had hoped that you would change your mind," he admitted. "Do you have everything that you need?"

Fidgeting in my seat I said, "Actually, there was something that I was hoping to ask you for."

"Oh?" he asked and leaned forward, linking his hands together and then leaned his chin on top of them.

"Would it be possible to borrow one of your horses for my trip? I would be sure to return it afterwards." Waiting for his response was nerve wracking. He could tell me no and there was nothing I could do about it. Aside from stealing a horse, but I doubted I would make it out of the castle.

"If I tell you, 'no', will you stay?"

I laughed and shook my head. "I'll still go."

He sighed. "I thought you would say that. Very well, I will allow you to borrow a horse. It will ease my mind a little to know that you aren't traveling on foot at least."

"Thank you!" I said happily.

"Promise me one thing?" he requested.

I nodded.

"Come back."

"That's the plan," I said with a laugh that I did not feel in my heart. Terror ran through me at the unknown ahead.

Greydon brought us out the most lavish breakfast I had ever seen before. I ate until I was full and then ate a few more bites until forcing myself to push the plate away. "That was so good," I whispered and rubbed my stomach.

Zydon swirled in black smoke and then appeared beside me. My chair moved backwards on its own and he bowed to me. "May I escort you to the stables to pick your stead?" he asked in a regal tone.

I stood up with my hand in his and said, "I would be delighted."

Zydon slid my hand up to rest on the inside of his bicep and then led the way, by foot, to the stables. It confused me why he would walk places when he could use his powers to teleport instead, but I had not asked him or Lars about it. Several Enki'l murmured as we walked past and a few waved, but there were some smiling giddily as we went by.

Why? What were they so happy about?

The stables were enormous, housing over one hundred horses as well as feed, gear, and full time stable boys. Five of the boys jogged towards us as we entered, all looked like teenagers, but I knew they were much older than I was.

"How can we help you, King Zydon?" Roy asked. Roy was the leader of the boys despite being the smallest of the group.

"I have agreed to let Celwyn borrow a horse for a trip she is taking," he explained.

"How far is the trip?" Roy asked and looked at me with a frown as he began to sort through the horses they had and which might be appropriate for me to ride.

"The ruins," Zydon explained.

Roy's gaze shot up and he looked at Zydon and then at me. "The ruins? The ruins?"

Zydon nodded.

"How much riding experience do you have?" Marsterson asked me. He was the breaker, the one who taught the young horses to accept a saddle and a rider. They called it breaking, but from what I had gathered, he was extremely gentle and calm with them.

"Not much," I admitted honestly. "I have ridden a few times, but I'm not skilled nad have not had professional training."

"If she is a Shifter, why doesn't she just shift?" Preston asked. He was by far the most inquisitive and had asked me hundreds of questions since I arrived at the castle.

"She doesn't have the training or stamina for such a long trip. If she is injured halfway there, she may not make it the rest of the way," Zydon explained for me.

"If I am separated from the horse, will it come back here?" I asked Roy.

Zydon tensed beside me.

"The horse should wait to try to reunite with you, but if you and the horse are separated for a while, yes, it should return to the castle."

I nodded happily. If I did not make it, for whatever reason, I wanted to make sure that the horse was returned to Zydon.

"She's ridden Elly," Zydon told Roy, "And there were no issues."

"Elly is your mare," Roy said in shock. "I would not consider loaning her to anyone."

"If you believe she is the best fit for Celwyn, then she may take Elly. You are the Stable Master, so I will leave the decision up to your judgment, but Elly is available for you to consider. I trust your judgment and opinions," Zydon said.

"I could not take your personal horse," I whispered to Zydon as the boys talked amongst themselves.

He smirked and said, "I ride my stallion the most and honestly I think you are the only female I have ever seen Elly get along with."

"That is true," Marsterson said.

"Can I talk to you, King?" Roy asked and walked a bit away from us.

Zydon walked away to speak with Roy privately. While they

talked, I went to the tack room and grabbed saddlebags and a sleeping bag that would tie to the back of my saddle.

"Alright, we have decided to allow you to borrow Elly," Roy informed me. "We will go get her and bring her here for you."

"Thank you," I said appreciatively.

The boys left and Zydon came to stand next to me.

"You did not have to loan me Elly," I murmured. His kindness seemed to have no bounds.

"I know, but I wanted to. She is a good mare and will keep you safe as much as she can."

A horse being able to keep me safe did not make sense, but I did not question or counter him on his statement.

With steady hands, he began to play with my hair, running his fingers through the strands and then curling them around his fingers. A sigh escaped my lips and I leaned into his shoulder. Having someone play with your hair was one of the best experiences ever.

"What are your plans?" he asked me while he continued to play with my hair.

"Go to the ruins. Find the reason I was sent there, or not, and then return here," I answered.

"If you get into trouble, tell Elly to 'go home' and she will bring you back here," he instructed.

"Yes, My King," I agreed.

He stiffened beside me, but said nothing. Why did it bother him to hear me say that? I was only trying to be respectful.

"She's tacked and ready," Roy said as he walked Elly towards me, fully saddled and gleaming as though they had just washed her.

He helped me put my saddlebags and roll onto the saddle and then Zydon boosted me up on to her back. Elly nudged Zydon's chest and nickered warmly. He stroked her head, admiration evident on his face, and then whispered into her ear. She bobbed her head and nickered as if agreeing to what he had just said.

"What did you tell her?" I asked him curiously.

"To take care of you," he said with a smile. The smile wilted and then he asked, "Are you sure that you want to go?"

With a nod as my reply, I gathered the reins and made sure my feet were in the stirrups correctly.

Zydon leaned up and kissed me lightly on the lips. "Stay safe and come back to me, alive."

"I will try my hardest," I assured him. He took a step back and then whistled. The front gate opened and the bridge lowered across the moat.

"Come on, Elly. Let's go on an adventure." She nickered in response and walked out of the castle and across the bridge. She increased her pace to a trot and then to a canter, her smooth stride eating up the ground as we headed towards the ruins.

CHAPTER EIGHT

Darkness settled over the land as I continued on my journey with Elly. She walked with her ears pricked forward, breathing evenly and calmly. Part of me wanted to turn on my music player with my earbuds in, but I knew that I needed to stay alert and aware of my surroundings, in case of impending threats.

An hour or so after the sun set, I found a place off the path to make camp. Elly found water nearby and drank from it while I laid out my bedroll and ate a strip of dried meat.

"I've never been out on my own," I admitted to her. "When I went on trips it was with my friends or my family. I probably only spent about two hours of my day truly alone."

Her ears swiveled in my direction as I spoke and she cocked one of her back hooves up, letting her hip drop as she relaxed.

"When I met the other Shifters, I was happy to find new friends. That happiness was short lived. Zydon has been a bright star in an otherwise dark night. He has been beyond generous and I will never understand why he spent so much time on me. Probably pity."

She snorted and shook her head.

Laughter bubbled up out of my throat and I lay down. "Good night, Elly."

THE MAP THAT LARS HAD GIVEN ME WAS NOT ONLY VERY WELL drawn and detailed, but he had also written me notes on the back. I thought I was lost or had missed a direction, but then there, in the distance, a massive stone archway announced my arrival at the ruins. The ruins before me were magnificent. Stonehenge had nothing on this place. It had obviously been a large rectangular castle. One of the walls on the side was still standing, it's height staggering compared to what a normal castle would have. Elly snorted and swished her tail nervously.

We walked beneath the stone archway and entered the ruins. It was quiet, far too quiet. Why weren't there any birds singing or bugs chirping?

"I'll be right back, Elly," I promised her and then shifted into a bird and flew up into the sky until I was high enough to see the ruins completely. There did not appear to be movement down there. That was both reassuring and not assuring as the silence still bothered me. Flapping my wings, I flew lower to the ground and circled the ruins twice before returning to Elly and switching forms again.

"I don't see anything dangerous," I informed her.

She snorted and shook her head.

"Stay here, girl. I'll go see if I can find the woman from my dreams." I patted her neck, took my backpack out of the saddle-bags, and headed inside the ruins. Crumbled stone covered the grounds, but in the center the main part of the castle loomed before me. Slowly, I shuffled forward, wary of finding a place where the ground was not as sturdy as it seemed and falling into a hole.

The door, which used to cover the entrance, lay on its face before me. At least eight feet in height, wood as thick as the castle walls, and carved with depictions of Shifters. It's twin still held its place covering half of the entrance, but it did little good since two feet to the right was a massive hole, large enough to walk an elephant through.

A large stick, similar to a walking cane lay to the right of the path so, I grabbed it and used it to probe the ground before me as I walked. Inside, I expected there to be ornate decorations, but it appeared that scavengers had come and pillaged everything that they could find.

"Celwyn," a voice whispered.

I spun around, searching for the source, but there was no one nearby. "Who's there?" I called, my voice wavering slightly.

"Find the necklace," the voice ordered.

The voice! It was the voice from my dreams!

"Where?" I asked. "Where is the necklace?" The grounds were so large that it would take me days or weeks or possibly months to search everywhere for a necklace. It had to be buried if the scavengers had not found it.

"Her chambers. She's trapped beneath the stones."

She? Who was this woman? What did the voice mean that a female was trapped beneath stones?

I gasped as I recalled my dream about trying to help a woman stuck underneath rubble. This was what it meant! Man, I was extremely slow lately. Hurrying, I made my way to the larger rooms, which looked like a bedroom. The first one I checked turned up empty. I hurried to the next room and began moving the rubble around in search of the necklace the voice told me to find.

"How do you expect to get The Devil of Olansia to concede these lands to us?" a male voice asked.

"It's not going to be easy, but these were Shifter lands before he took them," a second male voice, which I knew all too well. Chuck!

"It will take months to remove all of this rubble," the first voice said.

Moving faster, I searched the debris and just as the steps grew closer, I grabbed a square pendant and raised it from the rubble. It was silver with a ruby in the center with scrollwork along the edges.

The ruby glowed and then the woman whispered in my head, "You found me!"

"How much do you think it will cost us to get these lands from him?" the first voice asked again.

"You need to run! If they catch you, they will take you back to the Hall and you will not survive the week."

She was right. I listened to the sounds of their feet as they moved past the room I was in and continued on their way.

"Out the window," she ordered me.

The necklace was surprisingly warm against my skin as I put it on beneath my shirt. The window was open, so I did not have to worry about creaky hinges. I leapt out of the window and shifted into a large eagle, flapping as hard as I could with my backpack on.

"What was that?" the first voice asked from below me.

Banking to the side, I flew around the side of the castle and zoomed to Elly who pranced nervously. I shifted again and leapt up into her saddle.

"Hurry, Elly! Go home!" I ordered her.

She spun on her hind legs and leapt forward into a gallop.

I glanced back and my eyes widened at the wolf running after us. His eyes met mine and he slid to a stop, shifted, and yelled, "Celwyn!"

Turned back around, I leaned forward against Elly, trying to have little wind resistance and allow her to go faster.

"Wait!" Chuck called.

Not in this lifetime!

Elly continued her gallop until her sides heaved and her

flanks dripped with foam and sweat. After a glance back to confirm that no one was following us, I tugged on her reins to signal her to slow. She slowed to a stop and breathed fast and erratic. Dismounting, I also removed her saddle and bridle and led her to a stream I could hear nearby.

"You were amazing," I praised her. She nudged my shoulder gently and then buried her muzzle in the water as she drank greedily.

Sorting through the saddlebags, I got out her grain and found a good spot on the ground to put it where she could easily eat it. Next, I lay out my sleeping bag and then ate some food myself. Elly wandered over a few minutes later and devoured her food. Her body had steam rising from it and she shivered as a breeze blew past.

"I didn't bring any towels," I mumbled angrily. After searching through everything, I grabbed one of my shirts and used it to dry up as much of the sweat as I could, rubbing her body in circular motions to unstick her hair and allow it to cool faster. She would still be cold, but hopefully she would not get sick now.

"She's a smart horse," the woman in the necklace said.

I jumped, having forgotten that she was there. "Who are you? How did you get stuck in a necklace?"

Mist swirled in front of me and then a beautiful woman formed from it. "My name is Liana. I was one of the Five Celestial Tigers. When we sent Olansia to another dimension, it took all of my strength. I could sense that I was not going to regain my full power, so I used what I had left, and a little from my friend, to place myself inside the necklace. I knew that eventually the necklace would find its way to a deserving bearer, one I could help."

"You sought me out though," I reminded her.

She nodded. "You are a Shifter and as such, I am connected to you. I felt the betrayal you endured and your life ebbing as Zydon worked so hard to save you. You are the first Therianthrope in many years and it is a shame how Merle has treated you. The Shifters have fallen far from our former glory. If I were still alive, your existence would have been celebrated and I would have taken you in myself. Now, I can only hope to provide you guidance to live and prosper."

This was too much. Now there were ghosts talking to me.

"Go to sleep, child. Tomorrow we have a long journey ahead of us."

She was right, but that did not make it any easier for me to fall asleep. What was Zydon going to think? Would he accept it or would he tell me to get rid of the necklace? Should I? She seemed to simply want to help, but I had no idea if she could hurt me or not while locked in the necklace. No matter what trouble it would cause, I had to tell Zydon when I returned.

Twigs snapped behind me. I spun around and stared into the darkness, waiting for whatever it was to show itself. Nothing came. Had I imagined it? Being highly stressed did make the mind do strange things. Hallucinating sounds due to stress had happened to me before. Laying very still, I evened out my breathing and listened. The nocturnal animals called to each other softly, an owl hooted nearby and insects chirped. They were making noise, so I relaxed and tried to fall asleep.

When morning came, I felt terrible. My sleep had been fitful and I'd bolted awake every time there was a noise nearby. Elly looked ready to go and practically pranced as we started our way back to the castle. It made it a lot easier on me to have her already know how to return to the castle, because I could simply zone out and rest. A few times I began to fall out of the saddle, but Elly shifted her body and woke me up before I fell. Elly deserved at least ten bags of apples when we got back for taking care of me.

Elly took me a different way than I had come, her path taking me through a town, which was an incredible sight. There were vendors calling out for people to come see their items, children running around, dashing down streets and trying not to get run over, and men and women walking around with smiles. A few of the men had wings on their backs and though I wished to stay and stare at them, Elly continued moving.

An Enki'l I had never seen before headed towards me with a scowl. "Where did you get this horse?" he asked angrily.

"I borrowed her from King Zydon," I explained.

"Lies. The King doesn't let anyone borrow Elly," he spat.

"I'm on my way back to the castle right now," I informed him. "You can follow me and verify what I am saying is true then, if you would like."

"What are you?" the male asked.

"I am a friend of King Zydon's and have been living in the castle," I explained.

"You smell off," he said and then sneezed. "Something is not right about you."

I scowled at him and said, "You're pretty frickin' rude."

"We meet again," Adbalh said with a smirk as he walked out of a shop nearby and headed towards us.

I tugged on Elly's reins, but the Enki'l stopped her and held on to the reins. "You're not getting away from me."

"Please," I begged, "Let me go. I have to get back to the castle."

"You went outside of the castle without your protector," Adbalh said and stopped a few feet away. "You're either stupid or brave, but I'm going with stupid."

"Adbalh?" the Enki'l asked. "What are you doing here?"

"Shopping," he replied. "And you've brought me the greatest treasure of all."

"You have to run," Liana whispered.

I know!

"Elly, go home!" I ordered her.

She tugged backwards, trying to free herself from the Enki'l's grip.

"Oh, you aren't getting away from me this time," Adbalh said with a smile.

Zydon! How could I summon Zydon?

"You don't believe me," I told the Enki'l, "but if you summon Zydon or take me to him, he will confirm everything that I have told you. Please. Adbalh will kill me."

"Oh, my plans for you are no longer death. There are things that you can do for me that make you far more useful alive," Adbalh said walking closer.

"Not as long as I'm alive," Zydon said as he poofed into existence behind the Enki'l.

Adbalh hissed and then ran out of the town.

"King Zydon," the Enki'l said and bowed.

"Why were you holding her here?" he asked with a snarl.

"She is riding Elly," he explained.

"Did she tell you that I let her borrow her?" Zydon asked.

"Yes."

"Then if you had an issue or thought she might be lying, why not just follow her to the castle?" he growled. "You put her life in danger. Adbalh would have taken her."

He glowed with fury and clenched his fists closed.

The Enki'l released the reins and bowed. "I'm sorry. I did not know."

Elly trotted away, headed towards the castle and leaving Zydon behind. She ignored any command I tried to give her, but after a moment I decided that I should let her go to the castle. Zydon looked furious and had not even looked at me.

What had Adbalh meant about not killing me and keeping me now instead? What did he think that I could do for him or that I would even be willing to do?

The castle bridge was already lowered when I approached and when I entered the castle courtyard Lars was waiting for me.

"Are you alright?" he asked. He grabbed me around the waist and lifted me from the saddle.

"I'm fine, Lars. I am not hurt," I assured him.

"How was Elly?" Roy asked as he approached.

"She was perfect. She deserves a dozen bags of apples for keeping me from falling off her and alive," I told him honestly.

Lars took my saddlebags and ushered me towards the castle. "Come on, let's get you to your room so you can take a bath."

"A bath sounds amazing," I said with a contented sigh. The necklace swayed as I walked and I opened my mouth to say something to Lars, but then decided not to. If I talked to anyone about it, I needed to talk to Zydon first and foremost.

"Celwyn!" Jeff called with a wide smile as he held open the door to the castle. "Did you find what you were looking for?"

I nodded and said, "More or less."

"What does that mean?" Lars asked. "Did you find something?"

"Chuck was at the ruins," I admitted. "But I need to talk with Zydon about that first." Truthfully, I had forgotten about Chuck and what they had been talking about. It would be a good way to sidetrack them from asking too much about what I found at the ruins. Or more accurately, who I had found.

There was already warm water in the tub when we walked in. "Thank you," I whispered as I set my backpack down and headed towards the bath.

"I'll meet you in the dining hall after you've finished," Lars told me and set my saddlebags down.

"Yeah," I responded with a lazy wave of my hand. My clothes were sticky from sweat and it took a bit of finagling to get them off. I left them in a puddle on the floor and set the necklace inside them just in case someone came in while I was washing. Carefully, one foot at a time, I slipped into the warm water. As my chest slid down into the water, I released a loud and long sigh and closed my eyes. It always amused me that simple things like warm water were taken for granted by people, including myself, but one week away from it was enough to remind you how amazing it really is. I realized immediately that I needed to drain the water I had been in before washing myself. I drained it, refilled it, and then washed myself three times before I finally felt clean. I had no idea how people could handle being in worse situations like in the military or those living in third world countries.

As terrifying as this country was, it was better than some of the others I had seen.

My eyes were heavy, but no matter how tired I was, my hunger was even stronger. I dressed quickly and then rushed down the hallway to the dining hall. Zydon, Lars, and Jeff were huddled together, standing on the far side of the room when I entered.

I waved with a smile, sat down in my seat, and immediately began eating. Greydon walked out and his smile widened when he caught sight of me eating.

"You're looking well," he complimented me.

"Thanks," I replied and then shoved a bread roll in my mouth.

He set down a plate of chocolate chip cookies and said, "I thought these might make you a bit happier to be home."

Home. That word again.

"Thank you," I replied, teary eyed as I accepted his kindness.

"How are you?" Zydon asked as he sat down at the table.

Sniffling and wiping at my eyes, I answered, "I'm good."

"Then why are you crying?" Lars asked.

I shook my head. "I don't really want to talk about it right now."

"Lars told me that you saw Chuck at the ruins," Zydon said.

I nodded. "He and someone else were there. I did not recognize the other male. They were touring the ruins and discussing how they are going to try to get you to give them the ruins."

"Give them the ruins?" Zydon asked in disbelief.

"Yes, they want the ruins back since they were Shifter territory originally," I explained.

"What else did they say?" Lars asked while Zydon pondered over what I had said.

"They were discussing what they would have to offer you, but they had no ideas."

"Did they see you?" Zydon asked.

I nodded once and whispered, "But I was able to get away thanks to Elly."

"She outran a werewolf?" Lars asked in disbelief.

"Yes," I replied.

"Zydon, what are you feeding that mare?" Jeff asked.

Zydon laughed softly. "I've been telling you that she's an amazing mare."

"Out running a werewolf though? That's insane," Jeff whispered.

"Do you need a healer?" Zydon asked me.

He was trying to be a good leader, but it just pissed me off that he automatically assumed I would need a healer.

"No," I replied tersely. "I do not need a healer." The chocolate chip cookies were amazing, sweet and soft which was exactly how I liked them. I split the second cookie in half and watched the warm chocolate melt apart in a gooey delicious treat. The first half of the cookie was still warm and the second half I dipped in the milk that had appeared in front of me. Once I had finished the cookies, I looked up and realized that everyone was staring at me.

"I'm sorry, did you say something?" I asked and felt my cheeks heat in embarrassment.

"I asked if you found what you were looking for," Zydon asked.

Should I tell them? I rubbed the necklace through my shirt and debated what to do.

"Tell them," she said.

"I found a necklace," I told them and removed it. They stared at it intently as I set it on the table. "Liana is inside it."

"What!" Zydon bellowed and popped up out of his seat. Lars and Jeff moved away from the necklace and stared at it like it was evil.

"Can you manifest like you did the other night?" I asked Liana.

"No."

"You can speak to her?" Zydon asked.

"I can hear her in my head," I said and tapped my temple.

"How did she get there?" Zydon asked. He walked around the table and used some of his black smoke to touch the necklace.

"She said she knew she was dying, so she used the last of her magic to put herself in this necklace," I explained to them.

"Why did she seek you out?" Lars asked.

"Because she felt bad for how I've been treated by Merle and the others. She said she would have nurtured me if she were alive, so she wants to help me now," I clarified.

"There does not appear to be a curse on it," Zydon said and picked up the necklace. "There's not a spell to steal power of health," he said as he continued his examination.

"Is there a way to get her out of the necklace?" I asked. I had not thought to ask Liana earlier.

"Not that I know of," Zydon answered and shook his head. "She's stuck there permanently."

"Why would she want to live the rest of eternity inside of a necklace?" Lars asked.

"Helping our future generations and ensuring the continued survival of our race is the utmost importance to me."

I relayed her answer to them and waited as they silently deliberated over everything.

"It does not appear that she can control Celwyn or harm her in any way. If she really wants to help, it might be a blessing for Celwyn to be able to communicate with her. She could provide some insight or assistance in regards to dealing with the Shifters," Zydon said.

"So, I can keep the necklace?" I asked hopefully.

Lars and Jeff were both scowling, but Zydon nodded his head. "Yes, you can keep the necklace."

"We will continue to monitor you," Lars said, "Just in case things are not as they seem currently."

"Understood," I said with a nod.

"Did anything else happen on your adventure?" Lars asked.

Zydon was snarling when I looked at him. He said, "Adbalh had not left my territory yet and Johan stopped Celwyn because she was riding Elly."

"Adbalh was still here?" Jeff asked in disbelief.

"Did you kill him?" Lars asked.

Zydon shook his head. "He escaped, but Celwyn would not have been in danger if it had not been for Johan."

"He stopped her?" Jeff asked.

"He held onto Elly's reins to keep her from returning to the castle and despite Celwyn telling him that I had allowed her to borrow Elly and that he could follow her to the castle, he did not let her leave. She begged him to leave because of Adbalh and he continued to hold her."

"How did you know that?" I asked. "You weren't there and he had not contacted you yet."

"I am connected to all Enki'l," he told me and then looked away from me. "I would have come sooner, but I did not realize Adbalh was there until a moment before I arrived."

"You can listen in on all of your people's conversations?" I asked in disbelief. Talk about invasion of privacy.

"Yes, but I do not do it often," he told me. "I only did it because I felt your nervousness."

"Me? How could you sense me?"

"You were so close to the castle and to Johan," he answered, "That I was able to..."

"Wait, you said you could sense me all the time anyway. How? If I'm not an Enki'l?"

Lars and Jeff looked at each other and then at Zydon.

"What's she talking about?" Jeff asked.

"She misunderstood what I was saying," he explained, "I told her that I could sense when she was in danger."

"How?"

"We're connected," he responded vaguely.

"How?" I demanded. I was not certain why I was so adamant about getting answers from him, but I needed to know.

"What did you do?" Lars asked in a shocked whisper. "What did you do, Zydon?"

"What I had to!" Zydon bellowed. The ground and walls shook and the dishes clanked on the table from his yell.

Slowly, I backed away from the table and said, "You did something to me, didn't you? You changed me somehow."

"I saved your life," he reminded me. "I did what I had to in order to keep you alive. I could not just let you die."

"What did you do?" I asked.

"You're tired and you just got back," he said softly. "Now is not the time to discuss this."

"When will be the right time?" I demanded.

"Tomorrow," he promised. "I will tell you everything tomorrow."

I spun around and hurried out of the dining room before he could say anything else. My heart hammered against my chest in fear and nervousness. What had he done? How had he changed me? That female voice had said he was using an old spell or something to keep me alive. Was that what she had been talking about?

"Do you know?" I asked Liana.

She did not respond. Great.

Halfway through the night, sleep far from my mind, I walked out to the tree in the courtyard and sat down. What could it be? What could he have done to me? Was it bad? It had to be bad if he did not want to tell Jeff or Lars about it.

Despite the thoughts raging in my head, I fell asleep quickly and slept soundly through the night. At breakfast, none of the Enki'l were around. If I did not know better, I would think they were ignoring me. Oh, right. They were.

Breakfast consisted of the chocolate chip cookies that were left from the night before and milk.

"Sugary won't make him show himself," she chastised me.

"Oh, now you'll talk to me," I snapped. "How about while you're talking, you tell me what the hell is going on?"

Silent again.

"Typical," I grumbled. After dinner, with no one in the halls or anywhere I had been, I made my way outside to the courtyard. Expecting to find them sparring or practicing, I did not expect to find Lars fighting Zydon. More accurately, Lars punching Zydon and Zydon not defending himself. Despite how mad I was at Zydon, my body reacted before I thought about it.

"Stop!" I screamed at Lars and rushed forward. Lars did not stop punching Zydon who lay on the ground, his lip bleeding and several cuts open on his face which was swelling progressively worse. "Lars!" I screamed. He did not stop his barrage. He had to stop or he could seriously injure Zydon. Why wasn't Zydon protecting himself to begin with? I leapt forward, laying across Zydon to put myself between Zydon and Lars. "Stop!"

"Celwyn," Zydon whispered, "What are you doing?"

"Move, Celwyn," Lars ordered me.

"You are beating your King!" I shouted at him. "What is wrong with you?"

"Me? Me!" Lars shouted. He pointed at Zydon and screamed, "He's the one who has something wrong with him! He crossed boundaries that never should have been crossed. He promised he would never cross them again. Yet, here we are!"

"I had to," he whispered.

"No!" Lars screamed. "You didn't!"

"She would be dead!" Zydon screamed back. "I could not let her die!"

"Why not?" Lars asked. "What was so important about this girl that you had to keep her alive by using this magic?"

Me. They were talking about me and what Zydon had done to save me.

"What are you two talking about?" I asked. Leaning back on my heels, I looked from Lars to Zydon, one looking pissed and one looking ashamed.

"Lars, you don't understand."

"Explain it then," He spat.

No matter what Zydon had done, I could not believe that he was talking to his King in such a manner. Perhaps it was because they had known each other for so long. Perhaps the lines had blurred so that King and soldier and friends were not separate any longer.

"She's my other half," Zydon whispered.

Lars' anger ebbed as shocked replaced it. "What?"

"What?" I asked at the same time.

"She's my other half," he repeated.

"How long have you known?" Lars asked.

"I suspected the day I found her," Zydon explained while looking at his hands. "I knew for certain when Merle shot her with the Loup Dart and she began to die."

"Why didn't you tell us?" Lars asked.

"I did not want to say anything until I was certain and at that point it was already too late. Do you understand, Lars? I could not let her die. It was impossible for me to allow her to die when there was something that I could do!"

"Explain this all to me, please," I begged Zydon. "What do you mean I'm your other half? What is so terrible about the magic you used to save me?"

Lars bowed to Zydon and walked away, leaving us alone.

A few soldiers had come out to practice, but stayed a bit away when they saw us. Zydon's black smoke swirled around us and transported us to my room. He lay on the floor and stared at the ceiling.

Rushing to the bathroom, I got a bowl of water and towel to clean up the blood from his face. He lay still as I began cleaning his wounds, but then he gently grabbed my wrists to stop me.

His eyes were focused on me and he whispered, "You are new to this world. You do not believe in destiny or soul mates or your other half. There was so much happening to you beyond your control, I did not want to put this on you. Your reaction to this news may have been incredibly negative and might have endangered you."

"What you are saying is that you are my soul mate?" I asked.

"That term has negative connotations, which is why I prefer to use the term other half. With you here, I am more powerful, my soul feels complete, a heaviness that replaced the hollow feeling I have had since becoming an adult. You told me that you felt a connection with me, even before that day, did you not?"

I nodded.

"I could not let you die," he growled. "As you were dying, I felt that heaviness that I was growing to love, disappearing. I saw your light fading. I wish I had not had to do what I did, but I do not regret keeping you alive. I would do it all again to keep you alive."

"What did you do?" I asked him.

"There is an old magic, one we are not supposed to use. This magic gives part of myself to you and I take part of you into myself. By doing this, it allows me to not only be connected to you, but if I give you a direct order you have to follow it."

"You mean, that if you had told me not to go to the ruins, I would not have been able to go?" I asked breathlessly.

"Yes."

"Why didn't you?"

He sat up and released my hands, staring straight into my

eyes. "Because I did not do this to make you a slave. I did it to save you only. If there were a magic that could have kept you alive that did not have this other affect, I would have done it in an instant."

"So, I'm essentially your slave now?" I asked. "I have to do whatever you say now?"

"No, only if I give you a direct order, which I have so far tried to avoid."

No matter what he said, I had to obey his orders even if I did not want to. How could I even believe that we were soul mates or he was my other half? He could force me to believe now, couldn't he?

"Where are you going?" he asked.

I paused, not realizing that I had walked away from him. "For a walk," I whispered, "If that's alright with you."

"Celwyn," he whispered, "I would not order you around."

"Why don't you want me to call you, 'My King'?" I asked. "If I am your other half, then you are My King, right?"

"I don't want you calling me that because that is what those who made slaves of people forced them to call them. You are not my slave. You are my other half. You are…"

"I am nothing," I whispered sadly, "I am not an Enki'l. I am not a member of your house. I am a Shifter with no pack. Now, I am a slave with no king." Before he could respond, I left the room and walked down the hallways. What was I going to do?

"He is right about you being his other half," she informed me. "I can sense the connection between you."

"Perhaps you are feeling the magic he used to enslave me," I suggested bitterly.

How can I be his other half? Did that mean that I had to be with him even if I did not love him? Was there no free choice? Destiny was a joke. It was something that was used in movies and books, not reality. Fiction was reality now. Werewolves exist. Demon looking creatures exist. I could shift into any animal I wanted to. A woman was trapped in a necklace and speaking to me in my head.

Or, I was just insane. That definitely seemed like the more likely answer. It did not make sense that I experienced pain if it was a dream though. Insanity was more likely. Delusional, schizophrenic, and who knew what other diagnoses fit me.

The hallways did not ease my mind at all, so I went outside as well. The night's sky was filled with stars and a beautiful moon. The moon was so far away and so much larger than us. I was a small bug in terms of the universe. My parents would not miss me. The Shifters would not miss me. The Enki'l would not miss me.

"I would miss you," Zydon whispered from behind me.

"You can hear my thoughts as well?" I asked angrily.

"You could hear mine if you accepted our connection," he said.

"Maybe I don't want to," I whispered. I turned around to face him and folded my arms across my chest. "What if I don't love you?" I asked. "Do I have to stay with you?"

"You may not love me now, but you may in the not too distant future."

"What if I don't? What if I love Lars or Chuck or someone else?"

He froze, his eyes glowing and dark mist rose from body. "Do you love one of them?"

"As my other half, you would not be able to fall in love with someone else," he growled.

"What if I never grow to love you?"

"I would not keep you prisoner here," he said, "Though I hope you will stay."

"You could just order me to stay," I reminded him. "I have no free will."

"You do," he assured me. "I promise that I will never order you to do or not do anything."

"Make him swear on his title as King," she whispered.

His title? Why his title?

"Swear on your title as King," I ordered him.

He opened his mouth and then closed it. "I swear on my title as King, that I will not order you to do or not do anything."

He had done it?

"I'm shocked too. He must be very serious." She told me.

"I, uh." What was I supposed to say to that?

"I'm sorry," he apologized and picked up my hands in his. "Please, let me in. I know this is hard for you to accept, but you are my match and I cannot stand being away from you. It was incredibly difficult for me to let you go to the ruins, but I knew you needed to and so, I stayed here and stewed while you were gone."

"I just need some time to process everything," I told him.

He released my hands and exhaled, defeat on his face. "I understand."

It hurt to see him feeling so bad, especially after he had sworn to never order me around, but I needed time away from him. Without another word, I went to my room.

"Can you teach me to block him?" I asked Liana.

"Yes," she said, "Why?"

"Teach me."

"What do you have planned?"

"Teach me."

She sighed and whispered, resigned, "Picture the two of you standing in front of each other. Imagine a silver thread between you two. Then, build a wall between you two that squishes the thread beneath it."

I closed my eyes and did as she asked. As soon as I finished, I felt a change, a heaviness and loneliness that hurt. "Why does it hurt?"

"Because you aren't supposed to block each other," she snapped.

"Will this block his ability to locate me as well?"

"Possibly," she whispered.

"If I take off the necklace and stop touching it, will I stop being able to communicate with you as well?"

"What are you planning, Celwyn?"

"Answer me."

"No."

"Liar."

"Fine, yes, but I don't see what you could hope to gain..."

I slipped the necklace off and set it on my dresser. Completely separated from them, I knew it would not be long before Zydon came looking for me. I planned to travel without a horse, not wanting to get caught with Elly, so I did not have the ability to pack anything. The only thing I did pack was a small pouch of coins, money that Zydon had given me just in case I needed it. I was sure that I would need it.

I tied the pouch around my neck and then shifted into a large golden eagle. The urge to screech was hard to ignore, but I managed and flew up into the sky. The cool breeze ruffled my feathers and helped me fly higher and higher, it seemed like I could touch the moon, but I knew better. I angled myself South and flew away from Zydon and his territory.

CHAPTER NINE

I t took me half of a day to reach the boundary of his land. I flew along the border, somehow able to feel it despite not being able to see it, and debated my actions. Had he realized that I was gone? Surely, he had by now. Had he spoken to Liana to find out what I had done? She would not know where I was headed anyway, so I was not worried about that.

With a deep breath and a loud cry, I crossed the border and fell almost to the ground as pain gripped my chest. Why did it hurt to leave? Did Zydon experience this when he left his lands?

I righted myself, flew up again into the clouds and continued on my path towards the human cities. Once there, I was certain that I could pretend to be one of them and find my place among the other, normal strength beings. Here I would not be seen as a weakling. I could probably fit in here, maybe. Hopefully.

The city came into view and I was startled at the massive size of it. It was close to the size of my hometown. There had to be at least a million people down there. Outside of the city was a forested area, so I dove towards it to shift again into my human form. The forest was vibrant and alive with animals as I landed on the forest floor. It was peaceful and happy, so unlike the Werewood Forest near Zydon's castle.

I shifted and then remembered the cherry tree in his forest and the few moments we had spent together. My cheeks flushed as I recalled our kiss and realized that he had known then that I was his other half.

Shaking my head to clear the thoughts of him, I put the coin pouch in my pocket and headed towards the town. The streets were busy with people coming to and from the city, all smiling and happy as they went about their days. There were no walls around the city, the town just stopped, like they planned to expand it so they did not want to wall it in.

The main street led to a fanfare of vendors hawking their wares and items. The people smiled as I looked at everything, even if I did not buy something. I took a right off the main street and realized that I was in a clothing district. Perfect!

I examined each of their displays in the windows first and then chose my favorite to go inside. I had no idea how much items would be here, but I would be sure to make the money last. A woman in a pale pink dress smiled at me from behind a counter. She had sparkling green eyes and plump pink lips that matched her dress.

"Greetings," she said to me.

I smiled. "Hello."

"Have you been to my shop before?" she asked.

I shook my head. "This is my first time to the city," I admitted.

She clapped her hands together and smiled wide. "Wonderful! I am certain that you will find this city to your liking. A pretty young woman such as yourself is sure to find plenty of gentlemen callers in a short amount of time as well."

"Uh."

"What type of clothes do you need?" she asked and examined the worn clothes I was wearing.

"These are all I own," I admitted to her. "I had to leave my father's home because he was abusing me," I lied and looked at the floor. "I have some money, but I'm not certain how much I can spend here." Hopefully some compassion would gain me more than just money.

"Oh, you poor thing!" she gasped with hands up to her mouth. "Let me see how much you have."

I took out my coin pouch and showed it to her. She opened it and blinked in surprise. "Sweetheart, I thought you said you did not have much."

"I said I was not certain how much I could spend here," I reminded her, though I was surprised by her tone. Was the amount I had, a lot?

"You could buy my entire store with this pouch," she whispered to me. "Where did you get this money?" She raised her hand between us immediately. "Don't answer. The less I know, the better. Okay, let's get you some clothes."

"Could you recommend a hotel and possibly some place that might be hiring?" I asked her as she sorted out some clothes for me to try on.

"The Vixen Inn will be a perfect place for you to stay. My sister owns it and she is also looking for some help there. I will send you with a letter to help smooth the way. Do not show her your pouch. When she asks for money to pay for the room, only hand her the amount she needs from the change I will give you. Do you understand? One coin."

"How much is one coin worth?" I asked in disbelief. How could I pay for a room with just one coin?

"Most use copper coins as payment," she instructed me.

I looked at the gold coins in my pouch.

"One gold coin is worth one thousand copper coins. You can rent a room for one hundred copper coins a week."

"What!" I screamed. I had over fifteen gold coins. He had said it was just a small amount in case I wanted to buy something for myself. Fifteen thousand copper coins!

She nodded. "Well, clearly you did not know the value of what you have."

"I worked for a week with a man and he gave me this when I left. I was just a dishwasher, why would he pay me so much?" I asked in a whisper.

"He must have favored you," she said with a smile.

Duh.

"Okay, let's get you into the changing room so you can try all of these on," she said.

Four hours later, I left with two new suitcases filled with clothes and a bag of shoes. She gave me change back and then sent me on my way to the Vixen Inn with a letter she wrote for her sister. She had even sealed the back with wax and a stamp. It was so old fashioned and yet neat, that I loved it and wanted to have my own.

She had given me a hand drawn map to get to the Inn, but as I headed that way, I spotted a stationary store and stopped in. The store smelled like old paper and reminded me of how a library smelled.

"How can I help you?" the burly old man with a beard to his knees asked.

"I'd like some paper, a writing utensil, envelopes, wax, and a stamp for the seal," I requested.

"What would you like your seal to be?" he questioned as he went to the shelves behind him and began pulling out the items I had requested.

"Um…" I had not really thought about that.

"You can use your initial, favorite animal, or…"

"C. Please."

He put all of the items into a bag and said, "Four copper coins, please."

Four! So cheap! I counted out five and handed them to him with a smile. "Keep the change."

His eyebrows rose and he said, "Thank you."

Back on my way to the Inn, I found myself smiling wide, the tension I had been feeling gone. After two more turns, I realized that I was lost and no matter how much I scowled at the map, it did not provide me with answers.

"Lost?" a man asked.

I looked up and a male around my age, attractive with a strong jaw and gorgeous black hair, smiled at me. "Yes," I admitted. "I'm trying to get to the Vixen Inn."

"The Vixen Inn?" he asked and his eyebrows rose. "What are you doing there?"

"Looking for a place to stay as well as work. I was sent by recommendation," I explained.

"New girl in town, eh?" he asked and raised up on the balls of his feet. "I'll take you on over."

"Thank you," I said sincerely as I followed him.

"Want me to carry some of those bags?" he asked and eyed my load.

"No, thank you."

"I'm Tuck," he introduced himself.

"Celwyn," I replied with a wide smile.

"When did you get here?"

"Just today."

"I meant the island," he explained.

"I've been here," I told him, "I am from some ways away and ran away from my father who was abusive." It seemed like a good story so I would stick with it for now.

"I'm sorry to hear that you had to endure something like that," he said with a scowl. "Men should treat women with respect, not harm them."

"Thanks." I wasn't certain what else to say to him aside from that.

"Here we are," he said and motioned at a large inn with fancy doors. I could hear classical music playing inside.

"Oh, this is, um…"

"Swanky?" he asked.

I laughed and nodded my head. "Yes."

"It's one of the pricier inns, but does have great rooms."

"Thank you, Tuck, for helping me find it. I really appreciate it," I told him with a smile.

He smiled back and asked, "If I'm not being too forward, could I come see you tomorrow for a meal? I would hate for you to eat alone, without any friends in this town."

"You want to be my friend?" I asked, knowing clearly what he wanted. I wasn't some naïve child. I used to hang out with mostly boys before.

"I don't think she'll be needing your company, Tuck," Orion said from behind me. I knew it was him before I even turned.

"I think that's up to the lady to determine," Tuck said.

I turned and gasped. Orion still looked like himself, but he was more muscular and looked like he had aged at least five years. "Orion," I whispered.

"You know him?" Tuck asked.

"Yes, now please leave so I can speak to her," Orion requested.

"The offer still stands, Orion can let you know how to contact me," Tuck said and left.

Orion looked down at me and then enveloped me in a bear hug. I hugged him back, glad that he was okay. He released me and gave me his stupid smirk. "Hey," he said in greeting.

"Hey? Hey! Where the hell have you been?" I asked angrily. "Ronnie said your house was empty, like alien abduction empty."

"When magic returned, my family and I were teleported here," he explained.

"Teleported? Wait, what are you?" I asked him.

"I'm a mage," he explained.

"Mr. Johnson is too, but he stayed."

"He's older and stronger. He chose to stay."

"Oh."

"Why are you here? What are you?" he asked me.

I didn't want to tell him. I wanted to be human here. "Human, but my dad is a Shifter. Looks like I got Mom's genes through and through."

"If he is a Shifter, why are you here?" Orion asked.

"I ran away. I could not stand living with the Shifters." That wasn't a complete lie. I really did not want to live with the Shifters.

"Why were you going to the Vixen Inn?" he asked me.

"I bought some clothes and the owner there is sisters with the Vixen Inn's owner as well. The Vixen Inn is looking to hire some help so I'm coming to apply for a job."

"You, working?" he asked and then laughed loudly.

I punched his arm lightly and said, "Shut up." I was smiling since I didn't really mean it. It was so good to be near him again. He was my best friend growing up. More like family than anything else.

"I should let you get inside," he said. "Can I come meet you for breakfast?"

I nodded. "I'd like that."

After another bear hug, he waved and left. Orion, of all people to meet here!

The Inn seemed dead when I walked inside, but a twin to the shopkeeper came out. "Hello, how can I help you?" she asked politely.

"Your sister sent me," I informed her and handed her the note.

She pursed her lips in shock and read the letter, taking a very long time to read a one paragraph letter. "Well, it's nice to meet you, Celwyn. My name is Anla. Let's get you up to your room and then we can talk about employment. How long do you plan to stay?" she asked.

I shrugged. "I'm not certain. Can I rent it for a week and then let you know at the end of the week if I plan to continue staying here?"

"Very well," she agreed. "One week is one hundred copper coins."

I was glad that I had the change from my clothing purchases and gave her exact change. She smiled happily and pulled out a large bronze skeleton key that had a leather tag burned with the number ten on it.

"Room ten will be your room for the week. It is a lovely room with a balcony and a large tub."

"Perfect," I replied and followed her up the stairs. "Your inn is beautiful."

"Thank you," she said and opened the door with a ten on it. "I take great pride in my inn and work hard every day to ensure that it is clean and meets all of my guests' needs. I have been looking for a new maid, someone to wash laundry and dishes. Is this something you would be willing to do?"

I nodded. "I have some experience washing dishes for large groups of people." I doubted the humans here ate as much as the Enki'l did.

"Perfect. Meet me after breakfast is over and I will give you the tour and a rundown of the days' itineraries. Alright, I will leave you for the night to get unpacked and bathe. Welcome to the Vixen Inn, Celwyn."

Once she was gone, I sat down at the small desk in the room and began writing a letter to Zydon.

I am sorry for leaving like I did, but I want you to know that I am okay.
I left on my own and am safe and well.
Please, do not come looking for me.

Celwyn

IT TOOK ME AWHILE TO LIGHT THE CANDLE AND GET THE WAX TO melt right and I was disappointed with how my seal turned out. Nevertheless, I took the envelope down to the front desk where Anla was writing in a ledger. I set the letter on the counter in front of her. "How can I get this letter sent?"

"How far is it going?" she asked.

"To the Zitican Fortress."

"The Zitican Fortress!" she gasped. "Um, oh my. No one can deliver items to them. You will have to hire a mage to send it for you."

"Do you know where I can find one?" I asked. This was such a hassle to send a letter. How long would it take for them to adopt our new technology so we could just text or email each other?

"I will help you tomorrow, the mages are not available in the evenings due to mandatory meetings and trainings," she explained.

"Okay, thank you." Trudging back up the stairs, I realized that I should be able to ask Orion to send it for me.

Something in my heart throbbed unsteadily. I rubbed my chest and soon it eased. What was that?

IT TOOK ME A RIDICULOUSLY LONG TIME TO GET READY THE NEXT morning because I had so many different outfits to choose from.

"Yo," Orion greeted me as I sat across from him at a table in the large dining area where the other five guests were also gathered.

"Hey," I greeted back and set the envelope on the table between us. "Can you do me a favor?"

He laughed and shook his head. "Didn't take you long to use me for my powers."

After rolling my eyes, I explained, "I just need it sent. I can pay you."

"To whom?" he asked and leaned on his elbow as he chewed on a biscuit from the basket.

"The Zitican Fortress," I answered and quickly took a bite of my own biscuit. It was soft and buttery.

"I'm sorry, can you repeat that?" he requested and set his food down.

I glanced around to make sure no one else was listening to us and replied in a soft tone. "I need you to send this to the Zitican Fortress to King Zydon. Please."

"How do you know him?" he asked with a scowl.

I waved my hands. "I don't want to discuss it. Please, will you send it?"

He continued to scowl at me and then said, "It's going to cost you two copper coins."

Before he picked up the envelope, I set three coins on the table and slid them towards him. "An extra for meeting me," I explained.

He laughed and then picked up the envelope where I had written "Zydon" on the outside. "First name basis?" he asked and shook his head. "You'll tell me someday."

"Send it, please."

Holding the envelope between his hands, he closed his eyes, chanted a few words I could not hear, and then blue light covered him and the envelope. A second later the light was gone as was the envelope. "Done."

"Thanks."

"The Devil of Olansia, huh?"

"What?"

"That's what he is called," he explained.

"King Zydon is called, 'The Devil of Olansia'?" I asked in disbelief.

He nodded. "Yep. That's what my dad said anyway."

"Dad? Your dad died," I reminded him.

He shook his head. "No, turns out mom was hiding a lot of the story about my conception."

"Oh?" I asked curiously and leaned forward. "Do tell."

"A story for a story," he bartered.

I could tell him partial truths about how I ended up in the fortress and not about who I was to Zydon. "Fine."

He held out his hand. "Shake on it."

He always demanded we shake on deals and bets. "Fine."

After we shook hands, he explained that his mom had left Olansia right before magic left and when magic was getting ready to leave, she somehow stole some essence from his father. She held on to it until she was certain it was safe to have a child and then used it to impregnate herself and have Orion.

"So, your Dad had no idea you existed?" I asked.

"I knew as soon as he was born," a deep, booming voice replied. The man who walked in was Orion, but at fifty years old and battle worn. He was the hottest old man I had seen in a long time. He sat down at the table with us and held out his giant hand. "I'm Trevor, it's nice to meet you, Celwyn."

"How do you know my name?" I asked as we shook hands. His hand shocked mine, so I jerked it back and held it against my chest.

His eyebrows creased and he said, "I know quite a bit about you, more than my boy even knows."

"What?" Orion asked.

"I was meditating when a very angry Enki'l interrupted me," he explained.

A lump formed in my throat and it was hard to swallow. Crap.

"He could only send a projection of himself, but it was enough to send the apprentices running out of the hall," he continued.

"What did he want?" Orion asked.

"Celwyn," he answered simply.

"Why?"

"I think she should answer that," Trevor said and leaned back in his chair. "But first, I would like to know why you left."

"This is all crazy," I whispered. "Shifters and Enki'l who look like demons. Then they start talking about destiny and soul mates and I just couldn't handle it."

"Soul mates? Destiny? What are you talking about?" Orion asked.

I looked up at Trevor and said, "I wanted to be around humans. To be around others like me, where I did not feel weak or useless. I wanted to be somewhere that I belonged."

He smiled softly and said, "But you do not belong here either, Celwyn. You aren't one of them."

"I'm not like anyone," I admitted, "I have nowhere to go."

"You have a King going out of his mind with worry right now. He felt you leave his lands and contacted me in hopes that you had come to the city. He is worried about your safety and wants to make sure that you are okay," Trevor explained. He paused a moment and then said, "You belong with him."

"It's ridiculous," I snapped and shook my head angrily. "I can't handle it."

"Father, can I speak to you a moment, outside?" Orion asked him. "I'll be right back," Orion promised me and walked out with his dad. There weren't gone very long and when they returned Orion smiled at me. "Why don't I take you for a tour of the town?" he offered. "I can show you around and even take you to the Mage Temple."

"I have to work today and…"

"I'm sure that you can take one more day away," Trevor said.

"Why?" I asked suspiciously.

"I want to show you where I live and what I do," Orion admitted. "Please?"

There was something fishy going on and I really wished I knew what it was. "Okay."

"It was nice to meet you, Celwyn. You should join us for a meal before you leave," Trevor said.

"It was nice to meet you too," I replied softly and then added, "Can you tell him that I'm fine?"

Trevor nodded. "Will do."

"Come on," Orion said and held open the front door.

"I have to tell…"

"Dad took care of it," he informed me. "Let's go."

"Okay," I agreed and followed him out into the streets. There were a lot more people walking around this time of day and it amazed me at how happy everyone was. "Why is everyone so happy?" I asked Orion.

It felt so normal and natural to be walking next to him. We had been by each other's sides since we were toddlers. We had never been anything other than friends and it was so nice to have him around when all of the other boys were trying to find ways into my pants.

"They are happy because they are safe here and for the most part crime and violence are really low. There hasn't been a murder here for a very long time and the mages make sure to keep everyone safe."

"That is what you are, right?"

He nodded. "I'm a mage and I help keep the peace and keep everyone safe. It's been amazing, I have learned so much."

"What type of powers do Mages have?" I asked curiously.

"Our powers vary. The stronger you are, the more magic you have or the more types of magics you can do. I'm still pretty low in terms of power."

"Is your mom here?"

He nodded and then sighed. "She and Dad refuse to talk, so she's living across town."

"I'm sorry."

He shrugged and then smiled down at me. "Doesn't really affect me now that I'm living at the Mage Temple."

"Are there other new Mages that came from the US?" Did he have other Mages that he had to compete with?

"Yes."

"Do you have compete with them? Have you been in fights with them?"

He stopped and turned to face me. "What's going on? What happened to you that you aren't telling me?"

His Dad knew what I was, so it wouldn't be long until Orion found out as well. I looked at all of the people walking by and softly asked, "Is there somewhere we can talk privately?"

His brows furrowed, but he nodded and led me away from the crowded streets to a river that only had a few people randomly walking along it. He sat on the edge of the bank and waited for me to sit beside him.

"Spill. Everything, Celwyn. Everything," he ordered me.

"Promise that you won't stop being my friend?" I asked, hating that I sounded like a pathetic loser.

"I promise that no matter what happens or what you do or turn into, that we will be friends forever," he said and then nudged my knee with his. "Always."

I took a huge, deep breath and said, "My dad is a Werewolf, my mom is human, and I am a Therianthrope. A Therianthrope is a Shifter that can change into any shape that they want. Therianthropes were hunted to extinction by Adbalh Foxkiller, a Fey male, until I came along. He hunted them because pretty much everyone views us as threats."

"Threats? How are you a threat?" he asked and then smiled. "No offense."

"Because I can change into any animal and I can change into people."

His eyebrows shot upward and his eyes widened. "What? People? Like you could change into..."

I Shifted just my face into a perfect imitation of his for just a moment so he could see and then Shifted back. That gross feeling was so intense that I shuddered.

"Whoa," he whispered and leaned back to look at me. "I can see why you're a threat."

"Great," I muttered.

"Not to me. I know that you would not betray me. It just makes sense now."

"Anyway. The other new Shifters that I was training with didn't like me. I was a bit bossy…"

"Shocking," he mocked me.

"…And they did not like the fact that I was a Therian. So, they beat me and left me to die."

Saying it brought back fear and pain.

"How did you survive?" he asked and put his arm around my shoulders to comfort me.

"The King of Enki'ls, Zydon, found me in the forest and rescued me. He took me to the Zitican Fortress and helped me heal."

"The Zitican Fortress? No one has been allowed in there in over two hundred years," he said in shock.

"While I was there, my dad, Chuck, and the Alpha of the Shifters, Merle, came to the Fortress and demanded me. When I came out, I realized that the Alpha would not allow me to live. When I refused to return with them back with the Shifters, he shot me with a Loup Dart and I sort of, basically died. Zydon used magic to keep me alive and after, I started training with them. Then I had a run in with Adbalh and he tried to kill me. Zydon made a few advances, but a couple days ago he admitted that I was his other half, basically his soul mate. I found this necklace with a person trapped inside and she told me I had some destiny and blah blah. I just… It was too much, Orion. Not only was I a hunted Therianthrope that everyone wanted to kill because I was a threat, but now I was this ridiculously powerful and scary Enki'l's other half."

He was quiet for a little while, but eventually he whistled low and said, "Damn, Celwyn, that is a lot of shit to happen in such a short amount of time."

"You're telling me," I mumbled.

"Do you believe you're his other half?" he asked. "Do you feel a connection?"

"Maybe," I whispered. "But they can't be real, can they? Soul mates? People destined to be together? It's insane."

"There's a lot of insane things going on. I have magic, Celwyn. You can shift into animals. Your dad is a werewolf and my dad has crazy powers that you would not believe."

"For the first time in my life, I felt weak and useless, Orion. I hated it. I've never been one of those girls who worries about shit like that and now it seemed to only be about that. I could not even walk out of the castle without getting attacked."

"You're here," he reminded me. "You made it here to this city all by yourself."

"Yeah, because I flew."

"You need to straighten your spine. Since when does Celwyn look at the ground instead of meeting people's eyes? This is not you."

"I almost died three times," I reminded him. "I wouldn't survive longer than a millisecond against Zydon."

"That's not a bad thing," he replied honestly. "No offense, girl, but you wouldn't last more than a second against me now that I have my powers."

"Wonderful," I muttered.

"Would you rather be human?" he asked.

I nodded. "At least then I would have been able to fit in here with the humans. Now, I'm an outcast everywhere that I go."

"It sounded like you have a place to go right now. You have a male who would do anything to protect you and will provide for you until you die."

"What if he never loves me?" I asked softly. "What if he doesn't want to be with me or decides he wants to leave me later?"

"If he is truly your other half, then you two will fall in love with each other. You will become best friends and nothing will make you want to separate from each other. I've known you our entire lives and trust me when I say that any man would be lucky to have you."

"Yes, any man would be, but she's mine," Zydon growled and shoved Orion away from me. Orion slid along the river bank ten feet away from where he had been sitting.

"Zydon!" I gasped. "What are you doing?" I stood and started towards Orion, but Zydon grabbed my arm.

"Why did you leave?" he asked with a grimace. His eyes were pinched and he had one hand pressed against his chest. "Why are you here? Who is he?"

"He's my best friend!" I yelled at him.

"It's alright, Celwyn, I'm fine," Orion told me. Zydon turned towards him and Orion said, "I have no interest in Celwyn other than as a friend. I understand that she is your other half and even if I did have feelings for her in that way, I would never try to get between such a match."

"If you tried, you wouldn't survive very long," Zydon threatened him.

"Easy, Zydon," Trevor said as he walked towards us.

"How does everyone know where I am!" I growled.

"I followed Zydon," Trevor said and walked to stand next to Orion.

"Come with me," Zydon whispered.

I shook my head and backed away from him. "I just need time, Zydon. I..."

"I can't function while you are outside of my boundaries," he grunted. "It hurts worse than being electrocuted. It hurts even more with the wall you put up."

"How did you find me with the wall up?" I asked curiously.

"Our other bond," he said vaguely so that the Mages would not understand.

"Would you allow her to stay for one more night if I swear to keep her protected?" Trevor asked Zydon.

Zydon's body flickered, his body becoming see through.

"What's happening?" I gasped.

"This is just a projection," Trevor explained. "He is still at the Fortress."

"That's impressive," Orion said in astonishment. "To be able to physically interact with others while just a projection."

"King Zydon is one of the Five Celestial Tigers," Trevor told Orion.

Orion nodded as if he already knew that and he looked at Zydon with reverence.

"Please," Zydon pleaded with me. "Please come back."

"One more night," I requested.

He sighed and then turned to face Trevor. "One hair is harmed on her head and I'll burn the city to the ground."

Trevor nodded his head. "Understood."

"You won't do that!" I yelled at him. "Stop being ridiculous."

"I have to stop the projection," he told me. "Please, release the bond at least."

"I'll think about it," I promised. He tried to touch me, but his fingers went through my body.

"I will have someone pick you up tomorrow morning," he told me and then disappeared.

"He is terrifying," Orion said as he looked at his dad. "Is his presence even stronger when you are face to face?"

"Ten times at least," His dad replied with a nod. "He didn't obtain the title of Celestial Tiger by being weak. He was given the name Devil of Olansia after he defeated an entire platoon of Fey single handedly."

"Fey? Why was he fighting the Fey?" I asked. Maybe he had hated Adbalh before I came along.

"He was trying to assist the Shapeshifters because Adbalh was hunting them," Trevor explained.

"I thought he only hunted the Therinthropes?"

Trevor said, "He started with the Therianthropes, but then he became more twisted and began hunting every Shifer there was. He is the only reason that the Shifters survived after Liana died."

"She's not dead," I advised him.

Trevor blinked at me like I was dumb. "Excuse me?"

"She put her essence or soul or whatever into a necklace. It is...she is back at the Zitican Fortress. I found her in the ruins after she invaded my dreams to get me to come find her."

"She's alive in the necklace?" he whispered. "Would it be possible for me to talk to her?"

"Once I get the necklace back from Zydon's castle." I agreed.

"May we continue the tour?" Orion asked him. "Now that we have obtained Zydon's permission to have her stay one more night."

"Of course," Trevor agreed. "I expect to see you both for dinner at six o'clock. And Celwyn, you won't be needing to stay at the Vixen Inn. You can come stay in one of my guest bedrooms."

"But, I..."

"You heard Zydon. He never makes a threat that he won't follow through on. If anything happens to you, he will come and burn the city," Trevor reminded me.

"He will try." Orion said.

"No, he will do it. I told you, Orion. He is incredibly strong and if his other half is injured or far worse, killed, he will destroy every living thing within a fifty-mile radius of the city. I have seen it with my own eyes and do not want my son and wife to be killed as well as me."

"You know he is powerful and that he would kill you all, but you don't seem scared of him?" I commented. Normally someone would be terrified when describing a being as strong as Zydon.

He smiled and said, "Zydon and I are friends and we go way back. Though I do know that he could kill me. I also know that he won't. Unless it involves you."

"Can I take her to the Temple's meditation room?" Orion asked.

Trevor nodded. "I think she could benefit from it."

Orion dusted off his pants, which were still covered in dirt from Zydon shoving him aside, and once finished headed back towards the main part of the city. "Come on, I have a lot to show you in not much time."

"What about my stuff?" I asked.

"Dad's probably already sent someone to get your things and take them to our residence. He moves quickly and does not take no for an answer. He probably had it planned to ask Zydon to let you stay one more night as soon as he found out who you were."

"I like him," I told him with a smile.

He laughed and said, "I thought you might."

"So, you met Zydon, sort of," I commented. "Thoughts?"

"He loves you already."

"What?" I asked and stopped.

"His jealousy wasn't because you're his other half. His jealousy was because he genuinely cares for you. Also, he is in a lot of pain with you gone. What wall was he talking about?"

"I put up a wall that smooshes our bond so he can't hear my thoughts or track where I am," I explained. "I didn't want him to be able to hear what I was thinking all of the time."

"Does it hurt you?"

I nodded. "Yes, but it's a dull ache right now."

"He's probably taking most of the pain somehow," he informed me.

"He can do that?"

He shrugged. "If you asked me if King Zydon could lasso the moon I would tell you he probably could. No one knows his limits."

"Why do you know so much about him?" I asked curiously.

"We are taught about the greatest powers in Olansia so that we can learn to combat them and fight them. The last one we were taught about was King Zydon. We were instructed to never start a fight with him and if we did, we should be prepared to die because if he wanted to, he could wipe out every living thing from the entire island from his bed in Zitican Fortress."

"I know that he is powerful, but he doesn't feel that powerful," I told him. Maybe everything was just exaggerated by tall stories.

"You have some shielding from it because you're his other half," he explained. "Trust me, if you felt what we do, you would run for the hills screaming."

"Wonderful," I whispered.

"Hey, he is the perfect mate because he has every ability to protect you."

"Yet I almost died multiple times," I mumbled.

"Only when you were out of his protection area. If someone is stupid enough to threaten you when he is around, trust me when I say that they will not live long. His threat to me was one hundred percent accurate."

"You seem infatuated with Zydon," I teased. "Maybe you should be his other half."

Orion rolled his eyes at me and stopped in front of a bakery. "Want a cookie? This bakery has the best cookies I have ever tasted."

"Better than Mom's?" I asked with a smirk.

He nodded. "Even better than Mom's."

"Whoa," I gasped and hurried inside. "If they are that good, I'll need a dozen or more at least."

CHAPTER TEN

We met Lars at the border from the human's land to the Enki'ls land. As soon as he saw me, he rushed forward and raised my arms, spun me around, and then pulled me into a bone crushing hug. "You're safe," he whispered.

"Yes," I agreed and patted his back.

He pushed me out at arm's length and snarled. "Don't you ever pull a stunt like that again or I will hog tie you and leave you in your room."

I had not thought about Lars being worried about me. "I'm sorry that I worried you," I told him.

"I went out looking for you and spent all night out," he told me. "Zydon was ready to eviscerate Adbalh, thinking that he had gotten ahold of you."

"What did he do?" I asked.

Lars shook his head. "Let's just say that we had to remodel a few rooms after a few fits of rage."

"I'm sorry," I apologized again, more heartfelt this time and bowed my head.

"We all need breaks away occasionally. Next time, let me or Jeff come with you."

"Jeff?" Orion asked. "Who is Jeff?"

"Me," Jeff replied as he materialized beside Lars. A moment later Zydon materialized beside him in a swirl of black mist.

"Orion, I would like you to meet Zydon, Lars, and Jeff." I introduced. "This is Orion, my best friend from my hometown."

"Zydon, Lars, and *Jeff?*" Orion asked and snickered. "Really?"

"I don't understand what he finds funny?" Lars asked me.

Orion looked at me and after our eyes met, we both burst into laughter. "I know," I admitted to Orion. "I laughed when I heard it too."

"What are they laughing about?" Jeff asked.

I broke the wall within me, releasing our bond, and Zydon staggered a moment. I let him hear my thoughts about why we were laughing and after a moment he started laughing as well.

"I get it now," he said and then he straightened and smiled at me. "Thank you, for releasing the bond."

I walked over to him and motioned at him to lean down so I could whisper in his ear. "Can I invite them over to the Fortress in the future?" I asked.

"You could have just thought it," he reminded me.

"But I can't hear your thoughts for the answer," I reminded him.

"Yes, you may."

I turned around with a smile and said, "With Zydon's permission, I would like to invite Trevor, Orion, and Missy to Zitican Fortress for dinner and fun. I'm sure you guys can work out the dates that are best for you."

"Can you step over the border now?" Zydon requested.

I had not realized that even when speaking to him, I had stayed on this side of the border. Stepping over the border meant acknowledging that I wasn't human and never would be. It meant admitting that I would never fit in with the humans. It was admitting that I did not fit in anywhere.

"I won't abandon you," he whispered so soft that I was certain the other four, who were talking, had not heard him.

"What if…"

"I swear."

I gnawed on my lower lip a moment and then stepped over the border. Our bond snapped tight and I gasped at the same time Zydon did. "Why?" I asked him and felt even more connected to him than before.

"You're essentially an honorary Enki'l," Trevor explained to me. "As part of Zydon's House, you experience things as the rest of his House would. That means returning to your lands rejuvenates you."

"Weird," I gasped.

"Thank you for protecting her," Zydon thanked Orion. "And I apologize for my immature reaction yesterday."

"Nothing to apologize for," Orion told him. "And you never need to thank me or ask me to protect her. I've been doing it for twenty years."

I hugged Orion and said, "I can't wait to show you around the Fortress."

He smiled and said, "I look forward to coming."

"Thank you," I said to Trevor. "For everything."

"Anytime. I consider you family, Celwyn. You and Orion are like siblings according to his mother and I will view you as such from now on," he told me.

"Will you tell her that I love her and I'm sorry that I did not visit with her?" I asked Orion.

He nodded. "I'll tell her and be sure she comes with us to the Fortress."

I nodded and walked over to Zydon who was waiting patiently. Lars and Jeff had my luggage and waved before teleporting.

I looked up into his handsome face and said, "Let's go home."

A smile split his face and he wrapped me in his black smoke. "I hoped you would say that."

He teleported us to my room and kissed me. "I'm sorry that I frightened you," he whispered and kissed me again. "Please, don't leave like that again."

I kissed him back and said, "I'm sorry. I was being childish. I shouldn't have left like that."

"Promise that you won't run away again?" he asked and rested his forehead on mine.

I nodded and said, "I accept our bond."

An instant later my body exploded with heat and then I heard his voice like a whisper in my mind.

She's beautiful. I missed her so much. It hurt so much.

"I can hear you," I told him in a gasp.

"Through our bond?" he guessed.

I nodded.

It may be too soon for you, but I love you, Celwyn. I promise never to abandon you or leave your side.

I tried to keep the tears away, but they slid down my cheeks and I whispered, "Thank you."

"Are you hungry?" he asked. "I'm sure that Greydon will want to know that you are back and would love to make you some food."

"Yes," I answered, but then pulled him down for a kiss. "What did Trevor mean that I was an honorary Enki'l?"

"You are their Queen," he informed me.

"What!"

"As my other half, you are their Queen."

"I'm not an Enki'l and don't have powers," I reminded him.

"After we are fully united, you will have my powers," he informed me.

"Wait, huh?"

"I didn't tell you before because I figured that you would freak out," he admitted. "Once we are fully united, you gain the ability to harness my powers and borrow them or use them as you need."

"Won't that strain you and take away your available magic?" I asked.

He smirked and said, "I've got enough to spare ten others."

"So, you think you're going to have eleven soul mates?" I teased him.

"I only need, or want, one," he said and kissed me. "Seriously though, Celwyn, I have plenty of magic to spare. You could have destroyed that entire town while I was killing the entire pack of Shifters, and I still would have had spare magic."

"How powerful are you?" I questioned him. "Orion said they don't know if you even have limits."

"I have limits," he admitted. "But, it takes a tremendous amount to push me anywhere near them. It only happened once and since then I have gained more power, so I don't truly know my own limits now."

"How do we fully unite?" I asked. "I accepted the bond."

"Marriage is the next step," he informed me.

"Oh."

Zydon dropped to one knee and held up a beautiful ring with a shining sapphire gem. "Will you marry me?"

Tears sprang to my eyes and I nodded furiously. "Yes!"

He slipped the ring on and kissed me. "I love you."

"I love you, too," I whispered as I smiled up at him. "Forever."

He nodded. "Forever."

CONNECT WITH CATHERINE BANKS

I really appreciate you reading my book! Here are some ways to connect with me:
www.catherinebanks.com

Follow me on BookBub:
https://www.bookbub.com/authors/catherine-banks

Join my newsletter for deals and snippets:
http://catbanks.co/newsletter

Like my author Facebook page:
http://www.Facebook.com/CatherineBanksAuthor

Follow me on Twitter:
http://www.Twitter.com/catherineebanks

Follow me on Goodreads:
http://www.Goodreads.com/catherine_banks

www.Turbokitten.us
www.Turbokitten.us/catherine-banks

Purchase items handmade by Catherine:
http://Etsy.com/shop/TurboKittenInd

ABOUT THE AUTHOR

Catherine Banks is a USA Today bestselling fantasy author who writes in several fantasy subgenres under two pseudonyms. She began writing fiction at only four years old and finished her first full-length novel at the age of fifteen. She is married to her soulmate and best friend, Avery, who she has two amazing children with. After her full-time job, she reads books, plays video games, and watches anime shows and movies with her family to relax. Although she has lived in Northern California her entire life, she dreams of traveling around the world. Catherine is also C.E.O. of Turbo Kitten Industries™, a company with many hats including being a book publisher and Etsy store full of nerdy fun.

f facebook.com/catherinebanksauthor

twitter.com/catherineebanks

a amazon.com/author/catherinebanks

BB bookbub.com/authors/catherine-banks

MORE FROM CATHERINE BANKS

Song of the Moon (Artemis Lupine, Book One)
Kiss of a Star (Artemis Lupine, Book Two)
Healed by Fire (Artemis Lupine, Book Three)
Taming Darkness (Artemis Lupine, Book Four)
ARTEMIS LUPINE, THE COMPLETE SERIES

Pirate Princess (Pirate Princess, Book One)
Princess Triumvirate (Pirate Princess, Book Two)

Mercenary (Little Death Bringer, Book One)
Protector (Little Death Bringer, Book Two)

Royally Entangled (Her Royal Harem, Book One)
Royally Exposed (Her Royal Harem, Book Two)
Royally Elected (Her Royal Harem, Book Three)
Royally Enraged (Her Royal Harem, Book Four)
HER ROYAL HAREM, THE COMPLETE SERIES
The Demon's Fair

True Faces (Ciara Steele Novella Series, Book One)

Barbaric Tendencies (Ciara Steele Novella Series, Book Two)

Demonic Contract
Anja's Secret
Daughter of Lions
Centaur's Prize
Dragon's Blood
The Last Werewolf
Last Ama Princess
Transforming Rose
Lady Serra and the Draconian
Alys of Asgard
Phoenix Possessed
Tiger Tears
Sybil Deceived
Calvin's Alien Adventure
The Pawn
Stone Heart
Lonely Lioness

AFTERWORD

Thank you for reading OLANSIA. If you enjoyed the book, please consider leaving a review at your favorite book retailer.